LADY ROSE AND MRS MEMMARY

Persephone Book N° 53
Published by Persephone Books Ltd 2004
Reprinted 2008 and 2013

First published 1937 by Hodder & Stoughton
© The Ferguson Benevolent Fund
Preface © Candia McWilliam
Illustrations © Sylvia Salisbury

Endpapers taken from 'Masqueraders', a 1937 cotton
printed dress fabric made for the Calico Printers Association
© The Trustees of the Victoria and Albert Museum, London

Prelims typeset in ITC Baskerville by Keystroke,
Wolverhampton

Colour by Banbury Litho

Printed and bound in Germany by
GGP Media GmbH, Poessneck on Munken Premium
(FSC approved)

ISBN 9781903155431

Persephone Books Ltd
59 Lamb's Conduit Street
London WC1N 3NB
020 7242 9292

www.persephonebooks.co.uk

LADY ROSE AND MRS MEMMARY

by

RUBY FERGUSON

****

with a new preface by

CANDIA McWILLIAM

PREFACE

****

Scottish writing is in fighting form, here at the start of the twenty-first century. The list of real writers is very long, the list of famous ones scarcely shorter; some are, even, both. Most people who have heard of Irvine Welsh but not read him think of drugs and profanity; he is also a powerful listener and observer and a moralistic artist of urgent attention. His is a generation of impressive force and skill that includes Alan Warner with his lyric beauties and ecstatic journeyings, the unstoppable and original Alison Kennedy, Janice Galloway of the trenchant music. There are scores more, and younger writers coming always. Poetry is in great shape, Robin Robertson and Kathleen Jamie and Don Paterson prominent among the many makars, as Scots of old called their poets. James Kelman and Muriel Spark in their separate austerities preside. The shades of George Mackay Brown, Norman MacCaig and Sorley Maclean keep faith with the land and sea.

Most of these fine talents stop short in the main of addressing what you might call the middle class, leave alone the aristocracy, of Scotland. Ronald Frame, Allan Massie and Helena McEwen make their always interesting stands, but for those not already aware of the existence of such things, the contemporary reader might well gather that Scotland was a wild if lovely land of furious inebriates yelling the same short words again and again.

Not that the writers mentioned above represent such a world, but word-of-mouth has it that they do, and thousands of readers are cheated and deprived thereby, and the ancient ignorances between England and Scotland are massaged and fed and perpetuated.

What, on the whole, you do not get if you are English born and bred is the world of high Scots romance, the world to which the schoolgirls in Muriel Spark's *The Prime of Miss Jean Brodie* are raised, the beautiful hopeless Jacobite world of gesture and keepsake and heartbreak, a world that can so easily be travestied, that can topple just like that into kitsch, but a world that at its truest lies absolutely with the nap of Scotland's atmosphere and tone and sense of itself.

I must make it clear that it was in and to this world that I was raised, in Edinburgh, by a mother mad on Mary Queen of Scots. I was of course in love with Alan Beck Stuart of *Kidnapped*, by Robert Louis Stevenson. Stevenson himself had lived in the next street. Soon enough, we were visiting Culloden Field where the Highlanders were so cruelly defeated, and my mother was filling me with stories of failure and glamour while my father went about his vocation, the tracing and recording of the Buildings of Scotland, an enterprise that he died before finishing and that is perpetuated by dedicated souls similarly entranced to this day.

I apologise for so undisguisedly speaking of my own life in this preface. I do so in order to explain that it was disturbing and affecting to come across *Lady Rose and Mrs Memmary* and that I wolfed it up, since it is full of all those things that – not surprisingly – I do not often find out with poetry or memory – romantic description of Scottish great-house architecture, Scottish history of the most high-octane kind, innocent yet irrational Scottish patriotism, an account in unselfconscious terms of the physical beauty of Scotland. But what does it hold for the reader, you may reasonably ask, who is not quite so intoxicated by the North as I?

The answer is: a great deal. Because *Lady Rose and Mrs Memmary* is a very odd book indeed. It is a fairy story with an uneasy crash into social reality. It subscribes ravishingly to the deceptions and fatuities and wicked charms of the world in which it is set, the high aristocracy. And then, cruelly, and utterly convincingly, it shows the back of the canvas, and the harsh deals that hold up the whole lovely ideal. We are shown the hurt that is offered in the name of virtue, the neck-broken stupidity that keeps people purblind so as to protect property, the denial of instinct in order to guard the – fragile as we suddenly see – status quo. Nor do we lose sympathy with the cruel and limited who have so summarily shut out their victim, whom I cannot name or I should spoil this beautiful curdled high romance for you.

Published first in 1937, *Lady Rose* foreshadows much and celebrates as much that is soon to pass away, whether regrettably or not will be according to your leanings. It is lusciously overwritten in a yet weightless way, as though by a young girl in love defencelessly assuming that there surely is a happy-ever-after. It is a privilege to read this book now, later on after so much has happened to innocence, to childhood, girlhood, to the idea of marriage, indeed to the politics of Scotland itself. It seems impossible now that all Scotland might gather in as it were Edinburgh Durbar to honour a monarch.

And yet there is much that appeals to our preoccupations that have never gone away, for this book is about love and its price; even its prices.

Lady Rose herself starts life as a single radiant beloved female child of mountainous privilege; she is its sole heir. It is what she ends it as that makes this swift book for all its spangle and sentiment terribly painful and, in its preposterous way, at once all too real. This book contains a truly shocking letter. Through the worst blow a woman can sustain, Lady Rose achieves what we should all hope to before we die – understanding, humility, tolerance, grace.

She has changed through pain instead of cracking under it, as the brittle protagonists of what was really a fairy story might have. For this really is a fairy tale with all the savagery they invariably bear. No fairy tale is thornless; that is the point. This one simply drives home its sharp truth not metaphorically but by crashing together two worlds in a way that is oddly familiar to the reader. It's like waking up and wanting back the dream that had been so enchanting, and then, ruefully, reconciling oneself to the day ahead, that must be lived, and will be lived better in the light of the dispersed dream. Or perhaps it's like looking back on a time of peace, in a time of war.

I have tried, in writing these words, not to give too much away. Probably, as a good reader, you will have skipped the

****

preface anyway, conceivably one day to look at it long after you have loved the book.

I began to write down passages that might whet the reader's appetite, and found, as I only seldom do, that I was copying down the text. It is a very particular, unrealistic style, and quite high in sugar. If by any chance you are reading this before the book itself, do persevere. I am a dry reader, down on imprecision or what might be gush, and I had to take three jumps. Then I was in and there was no going back until I had finished and wanted at once to start again.

It's a little book about dreams and the hard world of money and position and their relation to one another. It's also a love story and a love letter - to Scotland or to a Scotland, one that will be there after the last nobles are dust and only the stars and mountains are left.

Candia McWilliam
Oxford, 2004

LADY ROSE AND MRS MEMMARY

Where is Keepsfield? Not upon the shores of Fife, nor upon any other Scottish shore. It never existed; it is an unsubstantial dream-house, built on air, a ghost of all the lovely mansions that stand memorials to the effulgence of the Victorian reign and the heroic story of Scottish character.

This is a work of fiction, and all the persons mentioned in it—with the obvious exceptions of Queen Victoria and Mr. Charles Kingsley—are fictitious.

Then old songs wake from enclouded tombs;
Old ditties sigh above their father's grave;
    .   .   .   .   .

And from the turf a lullaby doth pass
In every place where infant Orpheus slept.
Feel we these things? That moment have we stept
Into a sort of oneness, and our state
Is like a floating spirit's. But there are
Richer entanglements, enthralments far
More self-destroying, leading by degrees
To the chief intensity; the crown of these
Is made of Love and Friendship, and sits high
Upon the forehead of humanity.

KEATS : Endymion

CHAPTER I

M AY WE go up and see the house? ”
The Highland gate-keeper surveyed the strangers
from head to foot, appraising them.

“Aye, Mistress Memmary the caretaker will show ye
ower the hoose.”

The two men, Dacre the English lawyer and Van Elsen,
his American friend, editor of a New York gardening
magazine, had come to Scotland for a golfing holiday and
were already more fascinated by exploration than by the
game. In this they had been encouraged by Mrs. Dacre,
who joined them at Edinburgh and reminded them that
they were on the verge of the Scott country, and even
older realms of chivalry and romance.

“They worship two gods in this part of Scotland,”
laughed Helen Dacre; “Golf, and the Past.” It was true.
The smallest peasant child could handle a mashie and recite
you the Kings of Scotland. At ten years he could lay a
chip-shot dead to the pin; and confound you in argument

on the Casket Letters, and was James VI the son of Mary Stuart or the Countess of Mar?

On this August afternoon they had driven from Edinburgh to the shores of Fife, and, fascinated, had followed the windy, blue-lapped coastline for miles. At last they came to sand-dunes gay with sea-pinks under the soft blue sky. The breeze smelt of salt and honey, magically refreshing. Along the shore road they had been conscious for some distance of following a park wall; and now they arrived at huge stone gate-posts and wrought-iron gates, twenty feet high and bearing coats of arms in faded scarlet and tarnished gilt. At either side was a lodge. One was empty and dilapidated; at the door of the other stood a grizzled fellow watching the antics of a tethered goat.

A huge, newly painted board rearing up above the gates caught Dacre's eye.

"KEEPSFIELD"

Magnificent Residence TO BE LET Furnished
with Rough Shooting and Grazing Parkland

Apply
CRAWFORD, CRAWFORD & NICHOLSON
GEORGE STREET, EDINBURGH

"I'd like to see it," said Van Elsen. "What about asking the grim retainer if we may?"

"May we go up and see the house?" asked Helen Dacre. They were all conscious of the gate-keeper's shrewd appraisal; rather flattered by his implied approval when he said, "Aye, Mistress Memmary will show ye ower the hoose."

He unfastened a side-gate and they ran their car along a mile of carriage-drive, through a plantation where rabbits sat in the shaded roadway unafraid, hopping to one side to let them pass, and blackbirds sang a pure, clear song from the thicket; then across a vast park covered with grazing cattle and rows of pheasant coops. From here they could see the house, and it took their breath away.

It was a classic mansion of the late eighteenth century, glittering white, with pillared façades and sweeping terraces, standing in a formal garden to which long marble steps ran down.

"Oh! " cried Van Elsen. "Did you expect anything like that? How amazingly beautiful! "

"It is like one of those French water-colours that we saw at Versailles," said Mrs. Dacre. "Look! It hardly seems real; so still and gleaming against the soft olive-green of the park beyond, and that faint formal blue of the misty sky. There's a haze over everything. It is like a dream-mansion that as we go nearer will vanish in smoke."

"I hope not," said Dacre, pressing the accelerator. "I

say! What an enormous place. It's more than a mansion—
it's Buckingham Palace whitened, and in a better setting.
Look at the Ionic columns, and the height of those
windows. Terraces, balustrades, marble stairs. It must
have cost some nabob a king's ransom."

" But nabobs were nabobs in those days," said his wife,
" and workmen were slaves, and marble was as cheap as
human lives, and there were no land taxes. So this is the
entrance! " There was a great gravelled sweep with
statues of horses and warriors in marble and bronze; and
a central fountain where a Greek girl held out graceful,
appealing hands for the crystal drops which had ceased to
fall. A flight of steps ran to a pillared porch, guarding
double-doors of weather-stained oak, intricately and beautifully carved by the hand of a long-dead craftsman.

" It doesn't look," said Van Elsen, " as though it could
be inhabited, but the man said something about a caretaker. I'll knock. Say, will you look at the size of this
knocker? I feel like a bad man knocking at the gate of
Heaven."

Almost before the echoes of his knocking had died
away, one of the big doors was smoothly opened, and a
neat little old woman in black stood there.

" May we see the house? " asked Helen Dacre.

The old woman nodded. " Please to come in."

The hall into which they stepped left them dazed with

14

its beauty and vastness. It was all of mellowed marble, floor and walls and soaring horse-shoe staircase, and glimmered with a tint like the opening petals of a magnolia flower. There was a huge fireplace magnificently carved in the same creamy marble; a few classical statues, some suits of armour, and the life-size head of a boy in alabaster on a four-foot ivory pedestal.

" Upstairs is the main gallery," said the caretaker. " Will you come this way? "

" Wait!" said Dacre. " Whom does all this belong to? "

The old woman paused, one foot on the lowest marble step. She looked a tiny figure with her white hair and meagre black dress.

" It belongs to the Countess of Lochlule, sir."

" Oh! And where may she be now? "

" Well, sir, she has been on the Continent for a long time."

" Can't afford to keep up this place, I suppose? Taxes and depreciation and so on."

" Yes, sir."

" What a shame!" said Helen Dacre. " It is to be let, the notice-board said. How much do they want for it? "

" One hundred guineas a week in the summer, madam, and fifty guineas in the winter. It is partly furnished. They were hoping some rich American would take it."

" I'm an American," said Van Elsen with a laugh, " but I'm afraid it is outside my range."

" Do you realize," exclaimed Helen Dacre, the good housewife, " that all this marble will have to be washed every day? "

The old woman smiled faintly. "That is so, madam; I do it myself."

" Are you here alone? "

" Yes, madam, quite alone."

The twin staircases swept round to a gallery above, parquet-floored; with Indian rugs, priceless old wing-chairs of the seventeenth and eighteenth centuries, a few deep settees with loose brocade covers, and exquisite oil-paintings closely ranged on the walls. At either end of the gallery, french doors led out on to sunny terraces running the length of the east and west façades of the house.

Mrs. Dacre was exclaiming at the beauty of the furniture. The caretaker lifted one by one the loose chintz covers, and showed that underneath were hand-worked tapestries of intricate beauty and wonderful colour, or violet velvet upholstery sewn with gold thread and seed-pearls, or pure white silk brocade.

" But all these things are priceless! " exclaimed Dacre. " How can the owner be poor with so much of value? Or won't she sell anything? "

"She can't sell anything," explained the old woman with a patient smile. "According to Scottish law it is all entailed, for the heir."

"Then there is an heir?"

"Yes, the Countess's son."

"I'm not well up in the aristocracy," said Dacre apologetically, "so forgive me if I ask too many questions. Look, Helen, at that blue velvet chair with the arms and the high back. That looks comfortable and fit for a Queen."

"It belonged to a Queen," said the caretaker. "It came from Dunfermline where it had been the property of Queen Mary of Scotland. It was always known in this family as Queen Mary's Chair." She hesitated, and added, "Lady Rose used to sit in it many a time, and read to her children. Nobody has sat in it since."

"Who was Lady Rose?" asked Van Elsen.

"Lady Rose Targenet, sir. I should have called her the Countess, but I always think of her as Lady Rose."

"Oh!" cried Helen Dacre. "Were you here in the old days, when the family lived here and the house was in its glory?"

The old woman inclined her head. "Yes, madam. I've been here nearly all my life, since I was a child."

"Why then—you're all that is left of the past? That's almost too sad."

Van Elsen chimed in, " But you haven't any Scottish accent. That's odd."

" I've lived out of Scotland a great many years," said the old woman patiently. " Will you come this way, to the west drawing-room?"

She led the way through the double doors to a long and beautiful room into which the golden sunlight stole through the slats of the shady blinds. The blinds ran up softly under the old woman's hand and showed a vista of green, blue, white and gold beyond the four tall windows.

Dacre gazed around him at the vast, ornate room with its air of faded, silent grandeur.

" It must be my vulgar red blood," he said, " but I just couldn't feel at home in a room like this."

" That's a pity," said his wife, laughing, " because I was just considering taking all my money out of the bank and engaging a host of servants from an agency, and coming to live here in splendour for one week at a hundred guineas. I should love to."

" You're right, Dacre," said the American solemnly. " You have to be born to it. Think of flinging yourself down on that pink-and-silver settee with a tankard of beer and the *Sporting Times*—frankly impossible."

" Oh, but these are the state apartments," cried Helen. " You are absurd! The family would have cosy little sitting-rooms to relax in, wouldn't they, Mrs.——? "

"They call me Mrs. Memmary," said the old caretaker gently. "There is a very charming little sitting-room in the South Wing; it belonged to the late Countess."

"Another Countess?" said Van Elsen. "Are they all women in this family? Aren't there any Earls?"

"The last Earl died more than fifty years ago."

"Say," said Van Elsen drily, "let's get this straight. Who are all these titled people? We've got an Earl and two Countesses already."

"That's easily explained," said the caretaker in her placid, gentle way. "This house was built by the Earl of Lochlule in 1762, on the site of the old Keeps Castle. There was always an Earl and Countess of Lochlule living here until a little more than fifty years ago, and the title descended from father to son. The last Earl and Countess had no son and heir, only one daughter, the Lady Rose Targenet. When the Earl died more than fifty years ago, Queen Victoria made Lady Rose Countess of Lochlule in her own right, and gave the house and lands to her and her heirs for ever."

"And she's the one you call the Countess who owns this place and lives on the Continent? She must be an old woman herself."

The old caretaker nodded. "The Countess is nearly eighty. Would you like to see the state dining-room and the family portraits?"

"Wait!" demanded Van Elsen. "We're going too quickly. I want to get accustomed to the atmosphere of the place. Be quiet all of you!"

A hush fell. The lofty halls held that air of deep cloistered peace which belongs to Versailles and Hampton Court and other ghost-dwellings of the spacious, dead ages.

This transition to the atmosphere of another world is bewildering to modern personalities. The three strangers were conscious of a nakedness of spirit that made them uneasy spectators of a grandeur which was more than material. The old caretaker had slipped into the background, as caretakers do.

"Shall we go on?" asked Mrs. Dacre. "It's rather more like a museum than a dwelling-place, isn't it?"

"What is this room?" she continued, opening a door on the east side of the corridor, and then exclaiming at the view that met her eyes framed in the tall windows. She was looking straight across the level gold-green sweep of the park to a silver lake fringed with rushes and bright blue flowers. Beyond rose the bowing elms, an ocean of swaying green under blue August sky; and through a gap or formal avenue showed the gleam of an opal shoulder of distant hills.

The room itself was unfurnished and faded. The blue wall-paper was stained and had lost what must once have been a delicate hue, and the blue carpet was dull and trodden and showed signs of damp.

"I'm sorry," said Mrs. Dacre. "I see the room isn't for inspection. I suppose it hasn't had an occupant for many years, but it must once have been such a pretty room."

"It was a pretty room," said Mrs. Memmary, and with one finger she brushed the faded blue wall as though in a caress. "It was the Lady Rose's night nursery."

"Did you know her as a child?" asked Dacre, looking surprised.

"Oh, yes, sir," said Mrs. Memmary. "I knew her as a child."

Somewhere hidden away in the dusty portfolio of Time was a picture which fitted here. It was as though the Old Man with the forelock and the scythe was watching, with folded arms, that arrested moment when three tourists and an old caretaker stood in the silent and almost empty shell of Lochlule House, in the blue nursery which had belonged to Lady Rose as a child. So old Time seized his book and began to turn back the pages, ten, twenty at a time—more than seventy years of yellow leaves. Through them all the great white house gleamed whiter, and soon the Greek girl at the fountain was laughing as the waters of a bygone day gushed over her reaching fingers.

Time was moving . . . Time was retreating . . . Time was standing still . . . and the three tourists from England, looking curiously around that faded nursery, saw nothing beyond what their eyes showed them. Mrs. Memmary could have seen Time's picture if she had cared to look. Perhaps the Old Man nudged her elbow. She made no sign, though the portfolio lay open, and there was the picture in all its fresh colours with the sunlight of another century beating down from the sky.

1861

A little girl woke on a May morning in the prettiest bedroom in Scotland. It was her birthday and she was six years old. She had rather a long name for so small a girl, for she answered to the title of the Lady Victoria Elspeth Rose Grahame-Rooth-Targenet; but everybody called her Lady Rose.

She opened her blue eyes suddenly, and sat up in the silk-curtained bed.

She said, "Nana, Nana! I'm six!" Nothing was really different from yesterday, in spite of that tremendous and magical passage of time which had changed Rose from five to six years old. It was a large, lofty room with pale-blue walls sprinkled over with little sprays of primroses,

22

A LITTLE GIRL WOKE ON A MAY MORNING

tied with true-lovers' knots of yellow ribbon. The curtains
of the bed and the coverlets were pale-blue silk and the
window shades and carpet were a deeper blue. The carpet
had hundreds of little coloured flowers growing all over it,
nearly real enough to pick. The furniture was painted
white, and the dressing-table had triple mirrors and pale-
blue silk flounces and a satin bow, and two blue candles in
silver holders; just like Mamma's.

Nana, who was a big, bonny Scots girl of Fife, came in
and drew back the window-curtains. The windows were
twenty feet high and the glass was always sparkling clear.
Rose looked out and saw white clouds tumbling across the
sky, and the tossing tops of the great bowery trees in the
park.

"Oh, Nana, it's a fine day! Lovely, lovely! And I
don't have to do any lessons to-day because it's my birthday. I'm going to jump ever so far out of bed. Watch
me! One . . . two . . . *three* . . . ooh! Nana, dress me
quickly. I'm six. I can go to see Mamma in her room;
she said so."

Rose was dressed in her new frock of soft grey merino
with a wide rose-coloured sash and a rose-coloured ribbon
round her dark hair, brushed back from her brow. She
wore white socks and shining, ankle-strap shoes. She was
so excited that she could not keep still, and swung her
feet while patient Nana was trying to fasten the buttons.

Then she must eat her breakfast before she went to Mamma. What a bother! Breakfast was laid in the pretty schoolroom where a bright fire danced in the pink-tiled grate under the panelled wall, and Miss Macgregor was waiting, and Jean the schoolroom maid, and Douglas the under-footman. So Rose obediently ate her egg and a piece of toast, and because she was six was allowed to have milky coffee poured into her cup by Douglas out of his heavy silver jug. It was delicious to be six. Then presents. Three lace handkerchiefs from Nana, and a boy doll dressed in Macgregor tartan from Miss Macgregor, with a little velvet jacket and a bonnet and a real sporran, and actually a tiny dirk in his stocking.

And after breakfast Miss Macgregor took her hand and led her down the long, vaulted corridor hung with tapestries, where rather queer-looking marble ladies and gentlemen stood unclad at intervals to frighten you, to the South Wing; and knocked at the Countess's door, and let Rose in. Mamma was sitting before the window in a high velvet chair, wearing a lovely satiny-feathery robe.

" You said I might come," said Rose. " Have you had breakfast, Mamma? Look at my new dress. I had coffee for my breakfast. I'm six. Look what Miss Macgregor gave me. He's a Macgregor; Donald Macgregor. It's a fine day; it isn't raining the least little bit, and the lawns

25

look all shiny-bright. Oh, Mamma, *have* I got a pony and cart? "

Mamma held out her arms.

" Many happy returns of the day, my darling Rose. Mamma has bought you a pony and the prettiest little basket-trap you ever saw, and Johnstone will bring them round to the west door at ten o'clock to take you for a ride."

" A *Shetland* pony? Oh, do say he's a Shetland pony! "

" Yes, a Shetland pony."

" Oh, Mamma! Oh, thank you, thank you. I'm so happy. I'm all little bubbles inside. Mamma, I love you thousands of times. I love everybody. I love you and Daddy and the new pony and Johnstone and the Queen and Prince Charlie-over-the-water. Mamma, what are you going to do to-day? "

" Why, you funny little thing, I'm going to finish my embroidery this morning, and this afternoon I'm going to Edinburgh to visit Lady Leeson."

" Lady Leeson at the Castle? "

" Yes, of course."

" Oh, Mamma, take me! Take me! You said you would when I was older, and I'm six. I want to see the sentries, and where Queen Mary used to live. Mamma?"

" Yes, darling? "

" Have you always been one of the Queen's ladies?"

"For quite a number of years, Rose."

"Were you one of Queen Mary's ladies, Mamma?"

"Don't be absurd, child! She lived hundreds of years ago."

"You're just one of Queen Victoria's ladies?"

"Yes, dear."

"Shall I be one of the Queen's ladies? Mamma, is it *nearly* ten o'clock?"

"It's barely nine. Oh, Rose, what are you doing? "

"Just playing with your silver bottles and things, Mamma. May I use scent?"

"Well, just this once."

"What dress are you going to wear, Mamma? The lovely, rustly, greeny one? "

"Would you like me to? "

"Yes, please. You're very beautiful, aren't you, Mamma? Are you a little bit like Queen Mary was?"

The Countess laughed. "I haven't a drop of Stuart blood in me, Rose; nor an ounce of their fatal fascination. You silly little romantic thing! "

"May I go with you to Edinburgh? Please! "

"I don't know what Lady Leeson would say. A child of six! "

"I'll be good! I'll be good! I want to see Queen Mary's bedroom where they let the little baby Prince down the cliff in a basket."

27

" Oh, my dear child, you must let your governess take you to the Castle. Play with your pony, and don't bother me, there's a good little Rose. Mamma's darling! Look, the sun is shining brightly for you to take your ride in the park."

" Right to the end of the park, as far as ever I can see? "

" As far as you can see, where those tall trees are growing."

" Mamma, what is there over there, outside the park? "

" Well, where you are pointing, darling, is Edinburgh; and that way lies the sea where the big ships go sailing by."

" And *that* way?"

" Oh, that way are the mountains, the Highlands, where Daddy goes in the autumn to hunt the stags."

" Is it all beautiful, Mamma, all of Scotland? "

" Why, yes, darling; it is the most beautiful country in the world, and you must always love it dearly like the great men and women of the past who fought and died for it."

" Oh, I do, Mamma. And I cried for Queen Mary and Prince Charlie. May I go and see Daddy now? "

" You may ring for a footman, and inquire if Daddy is at liberty to see you. And don't stay too long or chatter too much."

The Earl was at liberty to see his daughter. Rose,

ushered in by a tall footman whom she did not know very well, stood shyly before the huge, carved, double-doors of the study. It was a magnificent room. The panelled walls were covered with pictures by famous artists, from the Middle Ages up to the present day. A great fire of logs burned in a silver grate under the high stone mantelpiece, the intricate carving of which had cost a craftsman his eyesight. Four tall windows with curtains of crimson velvet looked out on the formal garden with its lawns and terraces and beds of ·tulips. The great ceiling was painted with life-sized winged men, blowing horns. The Earl sat before his writing-table in a large chair of crimson leather stamped with a formal gold design of lilies and leopards.

"Good morning, Papa," said Rose, breathlessly. "Mamma said I might come to see you. It's my birthday: I'm six. Isn't it a beautiful morning, Papa? Are you very busy to-day?"

Papa took Rose on his knee. He wished she had been a son. Here she was, six years old, his only child. No boy; no heir. The ninth Earl of Lochlule was a blond man, inclined to stoutness, with eyes of the Lowland grey and splendid yellow whiskers. He stood six foot in his stockings, and looked a fine figure of a nobleman when he wore the kilt.

"So Rose is six! A great age. And Papa has a present for his little Rose. A netted purse, with six little tinkling things in it. You must ask your governess to take you to Edinburgh to spend them."

"Oh, thank you, Papa!" cried Rose, jingling the six pretty gold sovereigns, and burying a warm kiss in Papa's fair, tickling whiskers. "You are good to me. It is lovely to be six. I don't do any lessons to-day."

"I don't know that I approve of that," said the Earl frowning. "How well can you read?"

"Oh, *very* well, Papa. I can read anything, and Miss Macgregor and I are reading *The Lady of the Lake* aloud in turns. 'The stag at eve had drunk his fill, where danced the moon on Monan's rill.' I know it by heart. Am I a chieftain's daughter, Papa? Or is that only when you're Highland? Oh, and Papa! I've got a pony. Is it nearly ten o'clock?"

"You have a most disconcerting manner," said Papa, "of leaping from one subject to another. It suggests an uncontrolled mind. You must think more rationally, Rose. Do you write a pretty hand? That is important."

"Oh, yes, Papa."

"Then write me a little letter to thank me for my gift."

"Now? At once?"

"When you return to your schoolroom. I must leave you now; I have to make a very long journey to-morrow."

"I suppose you mean to London, Papa."

" Yes, to London."

" You'll see the Queen? "

" Yes, I shall see the Queen."

" I'm learning to curtsy very nicely for my presentation. I shall be presented at Holyrood, shan't I? "

" That event," said Papa, " is so far ahead that I think we needn't consider it for the present."

" What is England like, Papa? "

" Oh, just a poor, pale country, Rose. Not in the least like Scotland."

" And the English are very fierce and cruel, aren't they? Like Queen Elizabeth, and Cumberland's dragoons."

" You talk a great deal of nonsense, Rose," said the Earl. " You may ring the bell and have yourself conducted to your governess. Good morning, my child."

" Good morning, Papa, and thank you for my beautiful sovereigns. I hope you will have a very happy and glorious time with the Queen in England."

She had a splendid vision of a lady in scarlet robes, sitting on a high golden throne and wearing ropes of diamonds as large as pebbles, and a neat little sparkling crown on her yellow hair; and Papa, equally magnificently clad and looking very handsome, on bended knee, kissing the lady's hand.

" How lovely for Papa! " thought Lady Rose.

The pony was a darling, a small black Shetland with soft,

dark eyes and a mane and tail of spun silk. The little basket-trap just held Rose and Miss Macgregor and Johnstone; and when Johnstone had driven them once round the park, Rose and Miss Macgregor went alone and Rose held the reins. It was delightful. Then the pony had to be rewarded.

" An apple and some sugar," Rose demanded.

So a footman brought a silver salver with a rosy apple on a pink plate, and a silver fruit knife, and a small silver bowl of sugar, and Rose fed the pony, with little cries of joy.

" His eyelashes are quite two inches long," she exclaimed.

In the afternoon Miss Macgregor took her for a walk over the sand-dunes where she could see the glittering sea and the ruffles of white that the green waves carried. Rose skipped along tirelessly, with the fresh wind fluttering her hair under the brim of the little grey bonnet she wore. She asked a score of questions: " Miss Macgregor, how deep is the sea? . . . Is it the same sea they have in England? . . . When Queen Mary set sail for England, did she pass this way? Should we have seen the little boat from where we are now? . . . The other side of Scotland! What is it like there? . . . Do you like being a Macgregor, Miss Macgregor? Are the Macgregors a good clan like Lochiel and Macdonald, or a bad clan like the Campbells? . . . Why is it wrong to say that? Are there some good

Campbells? . . . Will you read to me to-night about Jason? May I stay up till eight o'clock? Is this all Papa's land? How much land has Papa? Is twenty thousand acres a great deal? More than Dalrymple has? More that Lochiel, or Gordon, or Dumbarton, or the Duke of Fife? May I pick these wildflowers, Miss Macgregor? May I take them home?"

She was the happiest little girl in Scotland. When it grew dark the crystal lamps were lit and the curtains were drawn, and Miss Macgregor read to her about Jason and the Golden Fleece; and presently Rose slid from her chair to the white bearskin rug and begged for a story that was true. And Miss Macgregor told her about Willie Douglas of Lochleven, and how he stole the keys of the castle and rowed the Queen across the dark, drear lake; and how the horses were waiting on the other side, with just a gentle chink of harness to tell that they were there in the shadow of the hazel thicket; and how the Queen made Willie Douglas mount first and ride at her side to be her page. And Rose's eyes grew large and dark, and her little heart thumped gently, and the ribbon slid from her soft hair and fell unnoticed to the floor.

"Good night, birthday," said Rose later, sitting up in the soft, white, silken bed under the azure curtains. "Good night, Mamma at Edinburgh and Papa in London. Good night, Queen Victoria and dear Queen Mary. Good night, my pony, and Johnstone, and home and everybody, and the good clans. And good night, dear God, and thank you for making everything so beautiful and me so happy; and forgive the Campbells for killing the Macdonalds if they are really sorry. Good night, Prince Charlie. Good night, World. I love everything; and I want it to be to-morrow soon. Oh, Nana, when shall I be seven?"

And for her youthful portrait take
Some long-waist child of Hudson's make,
Stiffly at ease beside a lake
                    With swans and willows.
                              AUSTIN DOBSON

CHAPTER II

"THIS IS the state dining-room," said Mrs. Memmary. "The table will draw out to seat sixty people."

"I suppose they often seated sixty people in those days," said Dacre. "Did they have banquets?"

"Oh, yes, sir, frequently." The old woman's lips melted at their corners into a smile, and her eyes had a far-away look. "The Earl was fond of entertaining, and they had large house-parties as well as the dinners when the Court was in Scotland. You see, sir, people hadn't so much to do in those days, and when you owned a fine house it was your pleasure to entertain your friends and show them your hospitality. And the cooking! You should have seen the string of footmen striding in with the joints on great silver trays. I remember how we used to hide and peep from behind doors to see the dishes go in. And to see the guests too, and the dresses and jewels and uniforms; because some famous people came to the house in the great days."

It was the longest speech she had made, and as though

afraid of having presumed by letting her tongue run away
with her, the old caretaker turned abruptly and began to
flick off specks of invisible dust from the carved clusters of
vine leaves and grapes which decorated the serving tables
in the alcove.

"By Jove, a musicians' gallery!" said Dacre. "I thought
those only belonged to the Middle Ages."

"I think it is a very good idea," said his wife. "Why
shouldn't the Victorians have had a string quartet to play
to them while they ate and drank? Actually the old Earl
was anticipating the modern cabaret-dinner."

"You're just irreverent!" said Dacre.

"I'm regarding the ancestors," said Van Elsen, waving a
hand towards the lofty walls, crowded with canvases of life-
sized portraits. "How many of these are Earls, ma'am?"

The caretaker turned gravely to the portraits. "There
were nine Earls of Lochlule, sir. Their portraits are all here;
and most of their wives and children too. This is supposed
to be the best portrait, a Lely: 'The boy Earl of Lochlule
and his cousin, John Rooth.'"

They stood back, and looked at the portrait of two lads
with glossy hair falling to their shoulders and framing dark,
eager faces, wearing green and russet country suits with
deep linen collars, and holding the leash of a straining grey-
hound.

Helen Dacre seemed to feel the gaze of dozens of painted

eyes staring flatly from pale, cracked faces or above cheeks
too ruddy, under brows that were shaggy or plucked and
arched, according to their period. And the rich, dark colours
of gown and doublet mingled to make a bloomy glow like
that which falls from a stained-glass window on a rainy day.

"The best pictures are in the next room," said the caretaker, leading the way; "we call it the cedar gallery. The
gentlemen used to come here after dinner to smoke their
cigars and look at the paintings." She smiled rather ner-
vously at the three visitors. "Perhaps you know a great
deal about pictures?"

"No, no," said Van Elsen. "Go ahead."

Dacre coughed, as though resenting his friend's implica-
tion of ignorance.

"The Earls of Lochlule had catholic tastes," he observed.
"What have we here? . . . Oh, but these are priceless; if a
little surprised to find themselves in a haphazard proximity.
Were all the owners collectors?"

"The last three Earls, sir, and they bought what they
fancied; I suppose the periods are a little mixed."

"Mixed is good. Tintoretto . . . Van Eyck . . . Raeburn
. . . Daubigny . . . Cuyp . . . *and* Constable . . . and
Bellini! But what richness for a private collection. Are
these entailed too?"

"Yes, sir. But in any case the Countess wouldn't sell
any of them."

" Oh, she wouldn't sell?"

" No, sir, not to see them go over to America."

Van Elsen blushed. " More marble statues standing around!" he exclaimed. " These public rooms are very museum-ish. Where would the Earl throw himself down, now, if he wanted a quiet shut-eye after lunch?"

" I can show you the study and the library," said the caretaker. " They are very fine rooms and comfortable ones too, but most people think them too dark for modern taste. People weren't so fond of sunshine in those days."

" Oh, no, Mrs. Memmary," cried Helen Dacre; " I'd rather stay here in these beautiful sunny rooms. I could never be tired of looking out of these wonderful windows. Oh, look, boys, look at that vista!"

The windows of the room in which they stood were planned to look straight across the vast lawns to an avenue of copper beeches, that led the eye down its narrowing length to where a marble column or monument gleamed pale at the farther end, nearly half a mile away.

" They called it the Bronze Avenue," explained Mrs. Memmary. " The column at the end was erected in memory of a favourite horse. The Countess used to say how she loved to see the sunlight on the changing colours of the copper beeches, as the year went from spring to autumn."

Helen Dacre found herself dreaming that she was disembodied; a radiant unclad spirit in the dawn of the world, tripping over that velvet corridor of dewy grass, between the bronze and gold and amber and copper pillars of those royal trees to the column half a mile away. There a white horse was tethered, with a soft muzzle and brown velvet eyes, a Pegasus waiting to soar with her to the overflowing sun. What a glorious place this was; what a magic place!

And suddenly, hardly knowing why, she found herself asking, " Did the little girl play in these gardens—the one you called Lady Rose? "

The old caretaker, taken by surprise, stammered that it was so.

Old Time, also startled, turned with unreluctant fingers to another page.

1865

It was very hot. The park shimmered in heat, and the grass had a bloom like the bloom of the peaches in Angus Cameron's hothouse. Rose did not like to think how hot it must be with the peaches and the pelargoniums and the pink wax begonias in the hothouse. The farthest trees were a bank of heavy mauve shadow, and under the nearer beeches and oaks were great blue pools of quivering shade, where the iridescent flies danced and the poor little hot calves lay panting. Even the lake did not look cool, for its silver was like molten metal and the rushes around it turned gold in the sun. The great lawns shone in vivid golden-green; you could see the hot air shaking and dazzling above the grass. The marble columns, the terraces, the broad steps were so bright and so white that it hurt to look at them. Thousands of pink geraniums seemed to blare their hot satisfaction from the urns and the balustrades. And over all went the brilliant sky, so filled with specks of scintillating light that you could hardly bear to lift your eyes to its infinite blue.

Rose had been having her painting lesson with Miss Macgregor, and she had executed—as Miss Macgregor called it—a neat, stiff little study of four purple pansies and a wisp of fern tied up with a blue ribbon bow. The paper had become rather limp and sticky, and some of the purple had run into the blue; but that was not carelessness on Rose's part, simply that the room was so dim behind the long drawn curtains of chintz lined with green silk that she could not see her work at all clearly. However, the picture was finished and Rose was rather pleased with it, and had signed it with all her initials. She would buy a little gilt easel for it and give it to Mamma.

At five, Colinby, the new English butler, brought Rose her tea. Rose adored this, for she was ten years old and Colinby was her first love; that is to say, for the first time she was appreciating masculine good looks. Colinby was

tall and slender; he had very blue eyes and a broad forehead
and lovely, well brushed silver hair. When Papa and
Mamma were at home Colinby served them, and Rose had
her tea from the hands of a footman, or even—the crown-
ing indignity to growing young ladyhood—from one of the
parlourmaids. But with Papa and Mamma away like this
she had arranged that Colinby should serve her tea in state,
and it gave her the most delightful feeling of importance.

After tea, however, she flung aside dignity and importance like superfluous garments. The next hour was her
own, and it was too good to waste. Her dress of white
muslin would do, and she seized a starched white muslin
hat and fidgeted while Nana tied it under her chin. Then
to the housekeeper's room to visit the kittens. There were
five of them, and Rose took them out in turns to see the
world and learn sophistication.

" They're so *sweet*, Mrs. Aytoun."

" Aye, it's the bonny wee things they are, your leddyship."

" I'm going to take the smallest grey one to-day, Mrs.
Aytoun. He doesn't really get much fun, because he's
little, and the big ones push so when anybody offers to
give one of them a treat. I shall give him the grandest
name of any; I shall call him Rob Roy, after the great outlaw chieftain. I think that will make him a happy, brave
little kitten."

Rose went out on to. the sun-drenched west terrace, cuddling Rob Roy, who by now wore a small pink silk handkerchief round his head to protect him from the sun. She sauntered along beside the high windows, blank before their lowered blinds; then step by step, slowly, down the thirty broad marble steps that led to the west walk and the level, shining lawns, and the delights of the spreading park. She described the scene as she went, to the kitten.

" You are at Keepsfield, Rob Roy," she said. " It is your home. All those dozens and dozens of windows have rooms behind them, and some day I'll take you all over the house; but when I only have an hour in the day to myself, I do like to spend it out of doors. Oh, Kitty, I love it; I love Keepsfield. It's the most beautiful house in all the beautiful land of Scotland." Adjusting the pink silk handkerchief, Rose made her way across the park. It was like wading through a lake of hot vapours, and when she reached the shelter of the trees she was panting a little and pushing the damp dark hair from her scarlet cheeks and brow. It was less baking among the trees, but heavily hot, and there were swarms of flies and all kinds of little creatures with shimmering wings and tiny whirring bodies.

Rose looked back at the house before plunging into the green depths of the plantation. It looked huge and white and noble against the pale, heat-blanched sky, with the olive-green woods beyond and the violet ridges of the Ochil

hills. So huge, so white, so fine with the long gracious lines
of it, and the ranks of high, glittering windows, and the
marble terraces, and the statues and the columns and the
glorious dignity of its pillared porches, and the sweep of
the carriage-drives and the tide of green lawns rippling to
the white foundations of it. Rose sighed with love and
satisfaction, and began to run through the trees. It was a
mile to the boundary wall. When she got there she felt
terribly hot, but she knew that a salty breeze from the sea
played on the other side and it was worth all the journey.
She tugged at the little green door in the wall. One of the
gardeners had kindly oiled the bolts for her. The kitten
whimpered and dug its tiny claws into her muslin sleeve.

"Ooh! Bother!" said Lady Rose.

The green door was open; she was outside Keepsfield.
She was in the great world; a little, dark-haired girl in
white muslin, looking very hot and not too clean, clasping
a grey kitten in her arms, standing on a winding white
road beyond which lay the sand-dunes dotted with sea-
pinks and the blue-grey tide of the receding sea. There
was a salt sea breeze, faintly, deliciously cool.

"Oh, lovely! Oh, heavenly!" said Lady Rose. The
kitten shut its blue eyes and buried its soft, heavy head in
the crook of her arm. A gentleman was coming along the
sea-road; middle-aged, and wearing a flowing cape. He
was bare-headed and had dark hair and side-whiskers, and

a broad forehead like Colinby's. His eyes were large and deep under heavy brows. Rose smiled at him shyly, one hand against the ivied wall of the park, ready to fly. He stopped. His face became full of light.

" A fairy! A fairy on the sea-road! Don't tell me you're real. And a fairy kitten too?"

Rose giggled. " I'm real. I'm too hot to be a fairy. And the kitten is real too. He's called Rob Roy after the outlaw chieftain."

" Indeed? Do you read Sir Walter Scott to the kitten?"

" I haven't done that yet," said Rose, delighted. " My governess reads to me."

" And what are you doing to-day in these wild regions, young lady? Exploring the country like myself?"

" No," said Rose. " I live here."

" Fortunate girl. God sent this country straight from Heaven and ready to use. Is this your garden gate?"

" Yes," said Rose. " But it's very hot in the park to-day. Two of the gardeners were mowing the lawn outside my schoolroom this morning while I was doing my lessons, and they nearly, nearly melted. I wonder what a gardener would melt into, don't you? Would it be an oily melt, or just a watery melt, like a fountain? I came out here because I like the sea breeze. It smells so lovely and exciting over the sand-dunes. I'm going to walk across the sand-dunes now to the edge of the sea. Will you come with me?"

A FAIRY! A FAIRY ON THE SEA ROAD AND A FAIRY KITTEN, TOO!

" With the greatest of pleasure," said the gentleman;
" but first I ought to introduce myself. My name is Charles
Kingsley."

" I like that name," said Rose. " Charles Kingsley. It
sounds like a brook running over little pebbles, and the
trout leaping, and Daddy's ghillie casting a line. It goes
tinkle-snap-tinkle. Shall I tell you my name?" Her eyes
twinkled mischievously.

" Oh, please do."

" Then get ready!"

" Why?"

" Oh, because it's a much *huger* name than yours."

" I shall square my shoulders," said Mr. Kingsley.
" Look, I'm all ready. Breathe the secret."

" Well, listen. This is it. Lady Victoria Elspeth Rose
Grahame-Rooth-Targenet."

" Oh, dear! Oh, dear! I shall swoon."

Rose giggled with delight. " Everybody calls me Lady
Rose. Or just Rose. And I'm ten."

" In that case you live at Keepsfield and your Papa is the
Earl of Lochlule."

" Yes. He's away. He has gone to London to see the
Prime Minister. I should like to go to London."

" You've been to Edinburgh?"

" Oh, of course! And Lord Glencoe lifted me right on
to Queen Mary's bed, in the middle of the red coverlet,

48

and Mamma was cross. And I played with the Governor's children at the Castle; we played tag. Mamma is in Edinburgh now. She is at Holyroodhouse in attendance on the Queen."

"Is the Queen at Holyrood now?"

"Oh, yes. She is having a drawing-room. I shall go there when I'm presented. Once I rode in the carriage with Mamma when the Queen drove through Edinburgh. Everybody bowed and cheered a great deal, but I had to sit very still, and my gloves were hot. I had a very tight hat-elastic too. It was awful. I'm glad I'm not Queen. I'd like to be one of the Queen's ladies, though. They have a lot of fun together. The gentlemen are very gallant, Mamma says, especially if you're pretty."

"Is Mamma pretty?"

"Oh, *lovely*. She has very sparkly eyes, and she looks like a bluebell dancing. The Queen is going on to Balmoral soon, and then Mamma will come home."

"You don't need to go to London," said Mr. Kingsley. "Edinburgh is much more romantic."

"Is it?"

"Yes. Even the squalor of Edinburgh is romantic and beautiful. You lose the dull present in the magic past. You are thinking all the time of the two whose spirits have set up a deathless reign in that city, lovely and royal to all eternity."

"Queen Mary!" breathed Rose. "Queen Mary, and—and—Charlie the Prince."

She danced on the sand-dunes.

"Now I can see the sea!" It was a blue, level tide running out to a radiant horizon. An old boat lay with broken bleached ribs in the froth of sea-pinks and pale, blown sand. Rose had seen it often, and made stories for herself about the heyday of that old boat and the men who sailed in her.

"Summer is so beautiful," she said.

"And perhaps," said Mr. Kingsley, "your life is nearly all summer?"

"Nearly all," agreed Rose. "You forget, don't you, when the sun is shining, that there ever was a time when you couldn't go out because of the snow?"

"You forget," he agreed gravely, "when the sun is shining. Would you like me, Rose, to send you a book that I have written?"

"A book?" Her eyes shone. "Oh, I should love it. What is it? I'll read it again and again. Do you really, write books?"

He nodded. "And this one was written for little girls like you. It is a fairy-tale about water-babies."

"Water-babies? I didn't know there were any."

He laughed with delight. "That is what I hoped when I wrote the book. Will you write and tell me if you like it?"

"Yes, I will. What time is it, please?"

He took out a heavy silver watch.

"Ten minutes past six."

"Oh, dear. I must go." Her dark eyes looked quite sad. "But, of course," she added, "the sea and the sun and everything will still be here to-morrow."

"I shan't be here to-morrow!"

"No." Rose looked puzzled.

"So I shall take your hand, child, and turn you to the sea—like this—and I shall say to you, read, and fill your mind with the wonderful history of Scotland; look, and fill your eyes with the glorious beauty of Scotland; dream, and fill your soul with the poetry and romance of Scotland; and let the love of your country be always in your heart, Lady Rose. And so good-bye."

"Good-bye. Oh, good-bye, Mr. Kingsley. And you won't forget the book?"

She held up the kitten. "Say good-bye to Rob Roy."

"Good-bye, Rob Roy," he said gravely. "May you grow up to be the flower of all the feline race."

"Perhaps," said Rose, "I shall see you again some day, in London or Edinburgh. Look out for me."

She was gone, running lightly over the pale yellow sand-dunes, the coarse grasses flicking her twinkling ankles; through the green door with a swift, backward wave of the hand; over the heat-baked park that longed and ached for the cool of evening. Back to the great white house, and the lofty rooms, and her own blue bedroom with Nana's grey room beyond.

A week later she wrote to her new friend in London; and ten years afterwards when he died the little letter was found in his desk.

KEEPSFIELD,
July 18*th*, 1865

DEAR MR. KINGSLEY,

Thank you very, very much for your book, *The Water Babies*. Miss Macgregor and I read it and we think it is a beautiful book. I wish Tom had fallen down my chimney, because I should not have screamed like Ellie, but I should have given him some food and kept him and made him happy, poor little Tom. But Miss Macgregor says that then there wouldn't have been any story. I hope there aren't any poor little chimney-sweeps now. There aren't, are there?

I loved the bit about the birds at Allfowlsness, and you wouldn't say where it was, but I think it is at the Bass Rock, because once we went there in Grandpapa's yacht, and there were thousands and thousands of birds, just like you said; and you said that their cry was like ten thousand packs of hounds and ten thousand peals of bells. And so it was. I shall read it again and again and learn some of it by heart. Thank you over and over, and many, many times, Mr. Kingsley.

From your sincere little friend,
·· ROSE TARGENET

... The children call, and I
Thy shepherd pipe, and sweet is every sound;
Myriads of rivulets hurrying through the lawn,
The moan of doves in immemorial elms,
And murmuring of innumerable bees.

ALFRED TENNYSON

CHAPTER III

HELEN DACRE sat on the low balustrade that
bordered the west terrace, and, taking off her hat,
felt the caress of the sun on her hair. This place was
exercising over her a strange magic; so far from the world,
so remote from the dusty ways of life to which she was
accustomed. This was a faery land, a realm of pure, bright
colour, of blander sunlight and richer air. Not peaceful
exactly, for there was a kind of tingling excitement in the
air, a sparkling flavour that you drew in with every breath.
It soothed you and yet thrilled you, because all your senses
were equally delighted at one and the same time; all your
five senses blessed with the loveliness of heaven and earth,
colour and scent, soughing sound of tree boughs and murmuring song of bees, taste of the sea-tang on your tongue,
cool, gracious pattern of the marble balustrade under your
hand, flowing classic lines of the white mansion under the
flax-blue sky. Mrs. Dacre closed her eyes, and still knew
herself to be in this paradise. Vaguely, many yards away,

she heard the burring of the men's voices. She could not
tell what they were saying; she did not want to hear for
fear of some chance word that might break her spell. She
thought, "I must capture this moment, so that I can have
a picture of it in my memory always. It will never come
again, and to-morrow I'm afraid that it will be no more
than a dream." For a few seconds she seemed to lose herself as though the sultry summer afternoon had overcome
her and lulled her to sleep; then she opened her eyes and
saw undimmed the green, the blue, the gold, the pure and
sparkling white. She was aware, too, that the old woman
was at her side, standing quite still with folded hands,
either patient or just complacent. She was a nice-looking
old woman, Helen noticed for the first time; slight and
erect, with a pretty head and soft, white hair. Rather an
indeterminate, unremarkable face, but eyes of a clear,
searching blue that gave you a level look and seemed
to see much farther than your countenance. Perhaps she
was Highland, this old servant, and had the mysterious
gift of second sight; or perhaps she was merely grave
with being so much alone and remembering departed
glories.

Helen watched a great cloud, like a heap of silvery
feathers, chase its own shadow over the lawns and sail on
joyously above the trees of the park. For no reason at all
she heard herself say,

"Have you—is there a picture of her? The little girl you called Lady Rose."

The old woman looked at her silently a moment. She unclasped her hands, and said, "No. There isn't any picture of her. You mean when she was a child, of course?"

"I did mean when she was a child. What was she like, do tell me?"

"Oh, she was just a little thing. Very happy."

"Was she pretty?"

"Not exactly pretty, except as all children are pretty if they're happy and sweet-natured. She had a bonny little serious face, and her hair was always tumbling in her eyes; dark hair it was, and her eyes were blue."

"Yes? Please go on."

"There isn't much to tell. What you'd notice most about Lady Rose was her happiness. She was that kind of child; everything was lovely to her. She always found something new to wonder at and delight in."

"Spoilt, I suppose? The only child in such a magnificent home."

The old woman shook her head slowly and smiled. "Oh, no. They didn't spoil children in those days. Her papa and mamma were very strict. Lady Rose was very fond of her governess, Miss Macgregor, and she had a passion for reading about the Scottish heroes. She had a

57

little painting of Queen Mary hung over her bed, and when she was only six she would kiss it good-night and weep for sorrow. She took things too much to heart, poor little Lady Rose."

" You were only a child yourself then, of course," said Helen Dacre. " Were your parents on the estate?"

" Yes, ma'am, and their parents before them."

" Really? And to think that you are the only one left here, when all the family and all the servants are gone, Mrs. Memmary!"

" Yes, ma'am." She moved a few paces away, and said, " There's a little miniature of the Countess in the cabinet, Lady Rose's mother. Would you like to see that? I could fetch it out here."

" Oh, please! I'd love to."

She was gone only a few moments; and returned quietly, holding out in her hand a miniature in a gilt frame headed by a bow of onyx and brilliants.

" That is the late Countess, ma'am."

" Oh!" said Mrs. Dacre. " She's *very* pretty."

" She was pretty; she was lovely, and very gay when she was at Court. She knew how to dress."

" At Court?"

" She was one of Queen Victoria's ladies. She attended the Queen at Holyroodhouse and sometimes at Balmoral."

"And Lady Rose, you say, wasn't like her mother?"

"Not at all, really. She was devoted to her mother, and made a kind of fairy princess of her. You see, in those days children saw very little of their parents. The Countess had dozens of soft, scented dresses, and little Lady Rose used to bury her face in them. She was always rather a baby for her age. That was why they decided to send her away to school."

"Oh, did they do that?"

"Yes. They chose a very good school in England, where a great many Scottish and English noblemen's daughters used to go. It was near Sandringham, and Queen Victoria took an interest in the school because she said it was there she grew her maids of honour."

"But did Lady Rose want to go away from this lovely place?"

"Want to! Oh, she cried and cried, and tried to hide her sorrow so that the servants shouldn't see and pity her. She knew it was the right thing and that she must be brave, but she loved Keepsfield so, and she could only thrive on the air of Scotland. She used to say she was going into exile, like some of her favourite heroes in history and romance."

"Did they miss her when she was away?"

"I can't say that, but she wrote to her mamma very often."

"Did she like England? What did she say in her letters?"

"I couldn't tell you, ma'am. No one ever saw them but the Countess and, of course, they will all have been destroyed years and years ago."

"Helen!" It was Dacre's voice breaking in. "Oh, there you are. Come and help me take some photographs. Luckily I brought a new film in my pocket, and this is a place you'll want to remember."

Unnoticed by any one a thin packet of letters had fallen from that portfolio of Time. The Old Man himself had scarcely noticed their loss, and as the wind of earth touched them they all changed to a fine white dust and were blown away across the park.

ST. ALMA'S COLLEGE,
NORFOLK,
September 20th, 1871

MY DEAR MAMMA,

I am really in England. All alone in England, and you and Papa and Keepsfield are far away. I keep telling myself that I am at school, like we have talked about so many times, but I can't believe it, and I keep expecting to wake up in my own darling room at home. But I suppose I *must* be finished and get to know other girls. School is so funny. Bells ring all the time, and you must do this and do that. We have history lessons with Miss North who is white-haired—but not old—and wears very tight shiny collars. I hate her very much, Mamma, for

she dared to talk about the Old Pretender and the Young
Pretender. Pretender, indeed! Some of the girls here are Scots
and some are English. The English girls have very neat hair
and long noses, especially Lady D——'s daughters, Isabel and
Una. Mrs. Challoner, the head mistress is very beautiful and
gracious, but she isn't really kind. I haven't liked any of the
lessons so far. Mademoiselle said that my French accent was
good. Apparently that is the only thing about me that is
good, because according to the other mistresses I don't know
anything about botany, or painting, or English history, or
playing the piano. Because I can play anything by ear, but
not arpeggios or studies from the book; and that is supposed
to be barbarous in England. But there are nice things here. I
share a room with the sweetest girl called Susan Jardine, and
she is so sweet and lovely and has brown eyes and fair hair.
Norfolk is very flat and ugly, I think. Papa said once that
England was a poor, pale country, and I think he was right.
But sometimes when the wind blows this way you can smell
the sea, and oh, it does remind me of the sand-dunes at home
and darling, beautiful Keepsfield.

Dear Mamma, I love my frocks, and the white silk is the
sweetest, or perhaps the brown with the little pink bows. It is
getting to be the fashion to wear hundreds and hundreds of
buttons. Please ask at Madame Fals in Princes Street, as I
should like to have a dress with more buttons than anybody
else. I am very happy, Mamma, and not being at all sad,
because it is all so interesting; and Queen Mary was a prisoner
in England for nineteen years, so I should be able to bear exile
too. My dressing-gown is red with fur edges, it is a fairy
princess gown and has a high collar. To-morrow we are to
have a lesson in ballroom dancing. Please may I learn the
Viennese waltz? Honestly, Mamma, it is not improper. The
gentleman stands quite a long way away and only touches you

with his fingers, and in white gloves. Of course we don't dance with gentlemen, only with the other girls. Mrs. Challoner said I must have your permission. All the girls do, so please, dear Mamma, say yes!

With love, I remain,

Your affectionate daughter,

ROSE TARGENET

ST. ALMA'S COLLEGE,
NORFOLK,

January 18th, 1872

MY DEAR MAMMA,

I had such a happy Christmas, and it seemed a long journey here in the snow. There is snow everywhere and the sky is hard and grey. It is cold at school, because discomfort is supposed to be good for our characters. We practise the piano in the morning before breakfast and our fingers are blue. The sun is always very red in Norfolk and not at all warm. Hunger sometimes seizes us because we have what they call plain food. I hate plain food. Is it good for me? We are permitted to have cakes sent from home, so will you please have them send me a *very large cake every week*. We are doing English literature and I love it. We read the plays of Shakespeare, and the most beautiful poetry of Shelley and Keats. Mamma, did you ever hear anything so lovely as this? I must write it properly with the correct punctuation. It is from Keats' Ode to a Grecian Urn.

> " Ah, happy, happy boughs! that cannot shed
> Your leaves, nor ever bid the Spring adieu;
> And happy melodist, unwearied,
> For ever piping songs for ever new."

Lord Byron was a very bad man, wasn't he? But I think he should be forgiven for all his sins because he wrote *The Isles of Greece*. And, oh Mamma, there is only one thing I long for in the whole world, and that is to meet Lord Tennyson. May I, some day? Would he ever come to Scotland? Would Papa ask him to stay at Keepsfield? And may I go to Grasmere some day and see the little cottage where Wordsworth used to live?

I have been playing indoor tennis. You don't mind, do you? It is quite a proper game, and I didn't show my ankles the smallest bit. It is great fun when the ball goes over the net and the girl at the other side can't get it back. I am very quick and I can hit the ball *hard*, and I don't scream when I miss it like Adelaide R——. Her mamma is one of the Queen's ladies too, but she—Adelaide—is so stupid and didn't know that there was a Court at Holyrood and that Edinburgh was much more royal than London. We have a singing-master called Mr. Anthony. We stand in rows and sing English ballads. In English ballads people never seem to do anything but gather roses and go to the fair. I should like to teach them to sing " Scots wha ha'e," or " Sing me a song of the lad that is gone," or " Who wouldna fecht for Charlie?" Mamma, does old Iain Macfarlane still play the pipes under your window on the anniversary of Grandpapa's birthday? I hope it will soon be summer so that I can come home. I think I shall die with joy when I cross the Border and see the sun shining on your side; on *our* side.

With love and love again,

From your dear

ROSE

ST. ALMA'S COLLEGE,
NORFOLK,
June 4th, 1872

MY DEAR MAMMA,

Yesterday it was very exciting. Who do you suppose came
to see us? You'll never guess so I must tell you. It was the
Queen. You know that Sandringham is very near, and she
came in an open carriage and brought the Princess Beatrice
with her. The Princess is the most lovely girl, I *think* about
as old as I am, and she wore a violet moire jacket and a large
white bonnet, and the *tiniest* slippers. The Queen is very
small, isn't she, Mamma? But *very great*. The Queen is god-
mother to Felicity L—— who was commanded to take tea with
her Majesty in Mrs. Challoner's drawing-room. And after tea,
what *do* you think! The message came down that I, Rose
Targenet, was to go to the drawing-room. I nearly died
with joy and heart-thumps. I had on my dark-blue silk
with the pretty lace ruffles that you gave me, and I tied a
dark-blue snood round my hair because it will not keep neat
like the English girls', and I went to the drawing-room and
curtsied most perfectly. And the Queen said, "So you are
Lady Lochlule's girl?" And I said, "Yes, ma'am. I am Lady
Victoria Targenet." And she liked that, and said to Miss
Challoner, "All these Scotch girls have the looks; and a kind
of braw independence. I like it." So she asked me if I enjoyed
school, and what I was learning; and I said that I loved
English poetry and Scottish history. And she said that she
hoped she would see me soon at Holyrood; and I wanted to
say, so did I, but I thought perhaps I had better not, so I just
sank down to the ground again, beautifully, in my *billows* of
blue taffetas. The Queen and the Princess both said, "Good-
bye, Lady Victoria" and I dare not say that I was usually

known as Rose! But it was exciting, Mamma, and I had to
write this special letter to tell you.

From your most loving,

" VICTORIA " (or ROSE)

ST. ALMA'S COLLEGE,
NORFOLK,
July 1st, 1872

MY DEAR MAMMA,

I am most dreadfully unhappy. I have had a letter from
Miss Macgregor, and since she left us she has not been able
to find another situation as governess. She is very *poor*, and
she lives at Peebles with her mother who is blind and very
poor too. Miss Macgregor has had to do needlework to make
a living, and nobody wants to buy her needlework, and she
has written to ask me if I will ask some of my friends to buy
it. Oh, Mamma, I haven't very much money myself; but
do buy all her needlework and send her a *lot of money*,
please! Enough, so that she won't have to be in trouble ever
any more. I can't sleep or eat, Mamma, until I know you
have done this. This is her address on a separate sheet of
paper. And will you find somebody quickly who wants a very,
very good governess?

From your loving
ROSE

ST. ALMA'S COLLEGE,
NORFOLK,
July 20*th*, 1872

MY DEAR MAMMA,

We had the most wonderful treat. I must tell you about it.
Mrs. Challoner took six of us older girls to London for three

65

days. My eyes *ached* with trying to see everything at once
and not to miss anything. We saw Buckingham Palace and
Westminster Abbey and the Houses of Parliament and some
fine shops. And then the most lovely thing of all happened;
we went to Keats' house at Hampstead and saw the room
where he slept, and the little, dark panelled room where he
wrote the Odes, and the tree on the lawn under which he sat
in the summer. And there were glass cases with his books and
his pens and his picture. And a lock of his hair! Lovely,
honey-coloured hair like silk. The attendant unfastened the
case and took the beautiful lock out and let me hold it on my
hand; and, oh Mamma, my hand shook and my eyes were
full of tears and one hateful girl *laughed*. But I have touched
his hair, his soft, beautiful hair that fell across his forehead
while he wrote " Thou wast not born for death, immortal
bird ", and I shall remember it as long as I live. I am so happy
because of this. I don't think I shall say any more in this
letter for fear of spoiling it.

Good night, Mamma,

With deep love,

From your loving

ROSE

ST. ALMA'S COLLEGE,
NORFOLK,
July 27th, 1872

MAMMA! MAMMA!

I am so excited that my pen is shaking and trying to run all
over the paper. It is the holidays on Saturday and I am coming home. I am coming home! Do you hear that? Oh, it is
so thrilling. It is a whole year since I saw Keepsfield in the
summer. I feel like Prince Charlie going to my own people

out of exile. Mamma, is my new room ready? And am I
to have a maid now instead of Nana? And may I go to
Edinburgh often with you? And is Papa going to Balmoral;
or shall we have people to stay, and shoot? I am bursting with
questions. For instance, can there be any joy in the world like
the joy of going back to Scotland from *England*?

Please thank Mrs. Aytoun for the iced cakes. The Lady
Rose's compliments, and they were the best cakes that ever
came out of Scotland. We ate one of them in *bed* which of
course is most strictly forbidden, but we were *ravenous* with
this plain food. I hope all the food in the holidays is going to
be rich and creamy and delicious. I'm greedy; I'm selfish; I'm
a barbarous little Scots girl ' wanting hame '. I can't think of
anything, but this time next week when I shall be at Keepsfield doing everything I like to do for six long lovely weeks.

With much love, dear Mamma,

Your loving

ROSE

ST. ALMA'S COLLEGE,
NORFOLK,
September 18th

MY DEAR MAMMA,

It seemed so strange and sad that you should be away at
Balmoral when I left home and not there to say good-bye to
me. I hope you are having a nice time. Thank you for the
photographs. I liked the one of Papa and the horse the best.
All the girls and I thought that Lady E—— was the stateliest
and the Princess of Wales the prettiest lady. She looks like a
Sea-King's daughter, doesn't she?

Lady Falconer came to stay with me the last few days and
bring me to school. She was fussy; but she gave me some

67

books and invited me to go and stay with her at Malcolm's Seat, may I? One day we went to Edinburgh and bought—please note—eight yards of pink satin brocade for me, six yards of black velvet for me, six yards of blue velvet for me, yards and yards of other things, all for dresses and so on and so forth for this greedy little Lady Rose; and a pair of the gayest pink slippers to dance in. They look as if they could nearly dance by themselves. Another day we went for a drive to an old ruined castle called Matho Castle. We climbed right up to the battlements, and we could look miles and miles out to sea, all blue and tossing and adventurous. Inland there was just a narrow neck of green field for a besieging army to approach, and we pretended one was coming, and I tipped boiling oil through the holes over the portcullis, and Lady Falconer was the sentry, and Giles and Margaret waved imaginary swords and shot imaginary arrows and we all shouted (only it doesn't matter, Mamma, because nobody could hear, honestly!). It was very warm and sultry weather the last week and we had tea each day in the rose-garden. The morning we left all the upper servants came to see me off, and Colinby opened both the great doors wide, and all the footmen stood on the steps just as if it were Papa going away; and as the carriage bowled down the drive I wanted to look back, and I couldn't. Because Keepsfield was so great and glorious and dazzling that morning, and so dear and sweet as well as being magnificent, that I should have jumped out of the carriage and run back to it all. Still, there was what Doctor Farquhar calls an " unholy joy " beneath my sorrow. It is my last term at school! I keep telling myself that it will soon be over; and then I will never go away from Scotland again as long as I live. Never, never, never, never, never! I painted some little water-colours down by the lake, which I think you will like, Mamma. The pink lilies are good, aren't they? I have put

the sketches on the Louis XIV table in your sitting-room. Oh
and I must tell you, the great big portrait of the Fourth Earl
fell down in the night and there is a hole in the canvas where
the corner of the dining-table went through. Giles Falconer
said it was an omen, like Birnam Wood coming to Dunsinane.
It feels very dull and cramped at school, but I am reading a
great deal, in fact in all my spare time. When Christmas comes
and I leave school I shall be nearly grown-up and ready to have
splendid times. Oh, Mamma, thank you for the white velvet
cape with the lavish fur; and will you please thank Papa
very much for the five pounds. And thank you, thank you
both for all my happiness and for letting me be your daughter
and share all your lovely things. I am truly glad that I was
born in Scotland. It would be awful to be English. All limp
and uninteresting like Charlotte Hampshire; and dreadful to
be Italian and *sticky-looking* like Maria Figlioni. I shouldn't
say that, it is unkind, but it is *rather true*. The bell is ringing
now, and that means we must march into the classroom and
repeat our French verses to Madame. Mine begins " *Au clair
de lune les fées s'amusent*," and I simply cannot remember any
more. I didn't learn it very well! French poetry is all rather
silly and passionless, I think, or else quite dark and gloomy. It
is never radiant and windswept like Shelley. The *second* bell!
I fly!

Your very loving,
ROSE

ST. ALMA'S COLLEGE,
NORFOLK,

December 12*th*

MY DEAR MAMMA,

   Yesterday was our Prize Day and Speech-making. The
Archbishop of Canterbury came to give the prizes and just to

69

relieve your bursting anxiety and to fill you with pride in your own talented child, let me tell you now that I won the school prize for French. When the usher called my name I was so surprised that I nearly fell down in a graceful heap in the corridor. Monica Stanley won the Queen's prize for deportment, and she was so nervous that she *tripped* as she went on to the dais, and Mrs. Challoner looked daggers at her. Two-edged dirks and claymores! It was fun going up for our prizes, just like being presented, and the usher rolled our names out so sonorously . . . " The Lady Victoria Grahame-Rooth-Targenet . . . The Lady Alison Vines . . . The Honourable Charlotte Greville . . ." and there were Rose and Allie and Lottie trying to look very serious and dignified and intelligent! My prize is a blue morocco leather diary with a lock and key so that I can write down what I do every day for a year. And then, Mamma, the Archbishop told us how fortunate we were to be at Mrs. Challoner's school, and that our schooldays were the happiest days of our life. I thought that a very depressing idea, because if you are miserable at school like some girls it is too dreadful to think that the rest of your life promises to be even worse; and if you are happy at school, then the prospect isn't any more cheerful! After many speeches we had the most delicious cakes for tea. Lady McConnell wants me to go and stay with them at Grasbury in the New Year, but I don't want to a bit, Mamma, so please make an excuse for me when she writes. Dinah McConnell is rude to the servants who can't answer her back. I hate her. So rapidly changing hate to love I hurl myself into your arms, Mamma, and say good-night.

From your loving all-French

ROSE

ST. ALMA'S COLLEGE,
NORFOLK,
December 18th

MY DEAR MAMMA,

This is the shortest letter that ever was. It is all over. I have been to school. I am finished. I am very nearly grown up. I am coming home! It will be very late on Friday night when I drive in at the gates of Keepsfield, and quite dark too, but the stars will be sparkling in the sky and by their light I shall see the "bonny hoose." I am glad Colinby is not leaving us to go to those English people; I don't want any of our servants ever to leave us. I can't imagine them ever wanting to! Well, Mamma, here is all my love. For Christmas I am bringing you a fire-screen I have worked myself in green and gold thread. Mrs. Challoner admired it so it must be beautiful. For myself I should like the gold brushes, thank you very much.

From your loving soon-to-be reunited,

ROSE

There must have been a great many more letters, but what happened to them all nobody knows. The Countess would read them hastily—when she had time—in that amused and tolerant mood with which parents do read the letters of their children at school; smiling at naïvetés, frowning at what she thought to be indiscretion or over-enthusiasm, and usually saying, as she folded the letter, what parents to-day are still saying up and down the Realm: "The child writes so badly; and, oh, her spelling!" Then the letter would be tossed aside, and somebody would put it into a drawer, and months later somebody else would tidy that drawer, and it would be: "What? Those old letters? Oh, throw them away. So much litter."

There were, of course, episodes about which Rose did not tell her mamma. Mammas of school-children to-day, also, know just as much as they are told. For instance, the incident of the music-master, Doctor Shand.

Mrs. Challoner's was a good school as schools went in those days; there was much of the convent and much of the prison about it. The governesses and teaching staff found themselves members of an abused, ill-paid, and down-trodden profession. They were poor, they were humble; if they exerted any authority at all it was by a domineering tartness of manner, bolstered up by a system which provided dire punishment for erring schoolgirls. Affection between governess and pupil was rare; there was more usually suspicion, if not downright animosity. As for the male members of the staff, they came under a different heading: they were—though down-trodden speci-mens—still Men, and therefore subject to suspicion not only by the pupils but by the excessively ladylike governesses themselves.

Doctor Shand was the music-master who taught the young ladies the piano in half-hourly lessons. The lessons were given in a small music-room, and a governess was always in attendance to ensure propriety of conduct.

It happened one day during Rose's lesson that Miss Clark, the governess in charge, was smitten by a disastrous attack of nose-bleeding, and gesturing wildly was compelled to rush from the room.

Rose felt light-hearted. It always annoyed her to play while from the tail of her eye she could see the stiff, grey alpaca shoulder of Miss Clark between herself and the window, and hear the snort of disapproval with which that lady would greet any remark not strictly concerned with sharps and flats.

Her hands dropped from the keys, and she looked appraisingly at the music-master. He was quite old, nearer seventy than sixty, and looked rather dusty. His hair was very thin, and he brushed long strands of it across his bald crown with a curious streaky effect. Rose wondered why, for it didn't make him look any the less bald. He cared a great deal about music; and wore a resigned and hungry expression, as though he had never had enough of anything he liked.

She said suddenly, " Doctor Shand, have you been teaching here long?"

He pushed down his spectacles. " Why no, Lady Rose, no; only a few months."

" Then you came here just before I did?"

" Yes, yes. . . . Now, Lady Rose, if you will kindly continue to play——"

73

" Oh, please, not yet. Not till Miss Clark comes back. Have you been teaching the piano always? Where did you teach before you came here?"

" Well, that was in Paris. I——"

" Paris! In a girls' school? Was it gay?"

" Not very gay, Lady Rose. . . . Oh, I do implore you to continue your playing! From the third bar . . . so! . . . No, it was hardly gay. I was there through the siege."

Rose clapped a hand to her cheek. " Besieged in Paris! By the Prussians! How dreadfully exciting. Do tell me!"

" But it was horrible . . . will you not play softly—so!— and I can tell you a little. You see, we heard the guns coming nearer; the firing, you understand. We thought we should be killed. The young ladies were convinced that the enemy would eat them."

" Horrors! Were the Prussians so uncivilized, then?"

" No, no. But in war anything can happen. Our armies were defeated—the French, I mean—the hospitals were full. They laid the wounded in the streets; in the street outside the school. There was blood in the gutters. The young ladies tore up their petticoats—oh, pardon me!—to make bandages. It isn't fit for your ears, Lady Rose."

" Yes, it is. Go on. Did——"

" Will you *please* continue to *play*!"

" And how long did it go on?"

" For months. We starved."

74

" Actually *starved*?"

" Oh, yes. We ate dreadful things. The bones of the
young ladies stood out of their faces. The people ate
rats."

" Rats! Ate *rats* in Paris only a year ago! And then
what happened? The enemy——"

" Alas, they won the war. Paris fell."

" They didn't—*kill* the young ladies?"

" No, no. But it was very bad. France will be revenged.
I hope I live to see."

" So do I!" cried Rose, forgetting the piano. " Now
tell me how you escaped and came to England, Doctor
Shand."

" But I didn't escape, Lady Rose. The war ended. It
was very sad. The French had to pay a huge indemnity,
and cede Alsace and Lorraine. I didn't care to stay in Paris
any longer, so I left and came back to London. Then I got
this post. But really, Lady Rose—to be talking like this
about myself—it cannot interest you——"

" Yes, it does. What was the war about?"

" Well, in the first place, they said it had something to
do with the Spanish Succession, but I think that was just
an excuse. One can always find an excuse for a war, you
know."

" Why should they want an excuse?"

" Oh, for the *glory*; the fine regiments, the bands, the

75

cavalry, the honours of war. War is magnificent, when you don't happen to be among the besieged."

"But somebody has to be besieged."

"Ah, but not the British. The British always win, so what does it matter? And the Prussians, they always win, too."

"But supposing the Prussians fought the British?"

"That's impossible. If we fight anyone in Europe we fight the French. *With* the Prussians; *against the French*. But with so many subject-races still to conquer in the East, British troops will win their glories far afield through your lifetime and mine, Lady Rose. Perhaps your happy Fate will be to marry a gallant soldier."

"That," said Rose, " depends on a lot of things. And I don't think ' happy Fate ' quite expresses what I feel about it. It sounds so inevitable. I would rather have a little choice in the matter. Oh, there goes the music! I'll pick it up. Tell me some more——"

"Lady Rose! Doctor Shand!"

At least three exclamation-marks of horror accentuated each name. It was Mrs. Challoner, the Principal.

The music-master, trembling, jumped to his feet.

"Where is the governess in charge?" demanded the lady.

"Her nose was bleeding," explained Rose. "She had to——"

" And why did you not come to me; or find another governess?"

" I—I never thought of it," Rose faltered.

The outraged Principal, in search of a scapegoat, turned on the helpless music-master.

" Doctor Shand, I am amazed at you; that you, a member of my staff, should countenance this indiscretion. I can only say that you are hardly fit to hold a position in an establishment of which propriety is the first essential. I have never been very satisfied with you. Now, having overheard your conversation with a pupil for the last few minutes, I am convinced that you are not only garrulous but doting. You are past your work; you may consider yourself dismissed."

The old man turned deadly pale. Even Rose who had seen little of the seamy side of life, realized something of what it meant to be turned out of employment at his age.

" Oh, Mrs. Challoner! I beg of you! Madam, please listen to me——" He faltered.

" Be quiet!" cried sixteen-year-old Rose, standing up with flashing eyes. " Listen to me, Mrs. Challoner. It was my fault. I made him talk, and you shall not dismiss him!"

" *I shall not?* Lady Rose, you are beside yourself!"

" No, I'm not. He was in the siege of Paris. He was telling me about it. I asked him to. I say he is not to be dismissed!"

The Principal was trembling with fury. "You impertinent, disgraceful girl. You are not only ensuring his dismissal, but you are almost within bounds of being yourself expelled from the school."

All Lady Rose's ancestors stood up beside her and fought.

"I shall be glad," she said. "Send me home. I'll go— and I'll take him with me and make him my music-master at Keepsfield. And I shall tell my Mamma how unjust you are; and I shall tell the Queen, and she'll believe me because she likes me!"

"You will go to the sick-room," said Mrs. Challoner, "and you will stay there during my pleasure."

Rose, not being able to think of anything else to say, and wondering whether she would really be sent back to Scotland and what would be Papa's reaction, allowed herself to be marched away.

The sick-room was a dreadful little dark place, with a narrow bed and a small window. Rose sat on the bed and waited for something to happen; but nothing happened, not even dinner. Tea-time came and went. She was horribly hungry. Heavens, were they going to starve her? Did they do that in schools? Did they actually starve people until they nearly died and nobody any the wiser? How long did it take to starve; for your bones to stick out of your skin like the girls in Paris? But they were doing

78

it for their country, and in company; not all alone in a horrible little dark bedroom that smelt of—of measles!

She could imagine she was in the siege of Paris. Imagination did a great deal to help pass the time away, and it was comforting to feel that at least there weren't any Prussians on the way to eat her. But rats! Eating rats. There might be rats in this room; and, Heavens, if you didn't eat rats when you were in prison *they eat you*! Bishop Otto, and the castle on the Rhine. Rose gave a shriek and hid her face in the faintly musty pillow.

Suddenly she heard her name in a low, excited whisper. She got up and ran to the window. There was a small hand on the window-sill, in the dusk, and a muffled voice said, "Quick! It's Susan. Open the window. I'll be caught, and I've brought you something to eat."

Rose, with the utmost difficulty, managed to shove up the window about two inches.

Susan Jardine's eyes appeared. "Are you dying of hunger? I know they haven't sent you anything, the beasts. Here's my apple dumpling; I saved it for you. I must fly."

"Oh, you darling!" breathed Rose. "I was pretending I was in the siege of Paris. They ate rats."

"Well, you can pretend this dumpling is a rat, if you like: it feels rather like one. It won't go under whole. I'll have to break it up. Do you mind bits?"

"I don't mind anything. I'm *nearly* a skeleton. Susan, what are they going to do to me?"

"Oh, don't worry. It will all blow over. Mrs. Challoner isn't going to let you go; it would be bad for the school, and she knows the Queen likes you."

"If she dismisses Doctor Shand I shall go."

"She won't. . . . But she'll torture *me* to death if she catches me, because I'm just a nobody . . . s-s-s-h!"

Lady Rose ate her broken dumpling, and, feeling a little better, went to bed and slept. Next morning she was released and sent to breakfast at seven with the other girls. No more was ever said about the episode, and Doctor Shand remained at the school. It was Rose's first realization of what it meant to be an important person, and the recollection of that night in her sick-room prison had its effect on her during the rest of her days at school. Who can say that it did not go further than that?

Perhaps in later years this memory may have influenced her, when for the second time in her life she defied authority, trusting to the power of her name and to the name of the Queen who "liked" her. But when *that* day came there was no open window; no friendly hand on the sill; no reassurance; no return.

Close not thy hand upon the innocent joy
That trusts itself within thy reach. It may
Or may not linger. Thou canst but destroy
The wingèd wanderer. Let it go or stay.
Love thou the rose, yet leave it on its stem.
Think! Midas starved by turning all to gold.

EDWARD BULWER LYTTON

CHAPTER IV

DACRE WAS fussing with a new Kodak film. He was always faddily particular how he put the film into his camera, because he said if the first wrapping round the spool was in the least irregular it would all stick when the film was half-wound, and there was nothing more annoying than to have pictures spoiled or wasted. So he was always very exact. Having charged his camera he began to look round for subjects and peep into his view-finder from this angle and that.

"This is good," he said. "I can get the terrace and the steps, and a shoulder of the house, and the large elm on the right to balance it and give a suggestion of the park." He clicked the shutter. "Now we'll go round to the front and I'll get a picture of the entrance and the Greek girl on the fountain."

He then suggested that his wife and Van Elsen should pose for him on the steps, but Mrs. Dacre demurred.

"No, we haven't the right."

" What do you mean?"

" That background, it doesn't belong to us. Why should we force ourselves into it, just so that we can have some pictures to show our friends at home of our smug little selves in the midst of unsuitable magnificence? I won't do it. You and Max can please yourselves."

This was rather an outburst from Helen, and coming closer she said to her husband in a low, confidential tone, " Sorry, dear, but I just couldn't pose on these steps, in front of that old woman; I haven't the right. I don't belong and she does, and what would she feel about it, remembering all the past and watching a lot of tourists looking as though they owned the place?"

" Just as you wish, Helen," said Dacre, " but you're probably reading your own feelings into her. I don't suppose she's as sensitive as all that. Tourists probably tip her well and she lets them have their money's worth. However, I've got six pictures, and now I should really like to get a time-exposure inside the hall."

He smiled at Mrs. Memmary.

" May I go inside and take a picture?"

" Certainly, sir."

" Do all visitors give you as much trouble as we do?"

Her lips curved slightly. " It isn't any trouble, sir."

" Do you get many visitors to see the house?" broke in Van Elsen.

"Quite a number, sir, mostly on Sundays. All kinds of people, you understand—bad and good."

"Oh, not many objectionable ones, I hope," cried Mrs. Dacre.

"Not many, madam, most people are very kind and interested, like yourselves."

"But we don't intend to take the house, you know; we couldn't afford it. I hope we are not here under false pretences."

Mrs. Memmary shook her head. "I'm happy to show you round. I like talking about the pictures and the rooms."

Dacre was by now discussing with Van Elsen the details of the proposed time-exposure. They went inside the marble hall again, and while the two men were finding a suitable support for the camera, Mrs. Dacre found herself once more by the side of the old caretaker.

"Please tell me," she found herself asking suddenly, "what did Lady Rose do when she came home from school?"

"Why do you ask that?"

"Because I'm imaginative, I suppose, and I pictured the great day, and these hall doors slowly opening, and the servants running forward eagerly; and the Countess in a lovely sweeping gown at the head of the staircase, looking down for her daughter; and then a very gay, fresh voice as

Lady Rose ran in. Do you remember it? Was it like that? "

The old lady looked at her curiously.

" It was—just like that. I remember it as though it were yesterday."

" And what happened next? "

" Why, the presentation. Lady Rose was presented, with all the other Scottish girls, to the Queen at Holyroodhouse."

" How magnificent! What did she wear? I don't know why—but I'm so interested."

" Have you seen the state apartments at Holyroodhouse, madam?"

" Yes, only two days ago."

" Then you'll have seen the Throne Room. You'll be able to picture the scene for yourself."

Helen Dacre smiled gently. " Of course you couldn't know what it was really like, any more than I could. I've never been within a hundred miles of being presented at Court. My father was just a hard-working doctor in an English industrial town, and my husband is junior partner in a law firm. But was her dress lovely; do tell me?"

That dress. Old Time was frowning and turning his pages. Where was it, among all these fluttering leaves? A great many pages went to make up the tale of sixty years; but one by one they fell from his old fingers like snowflakes, and the snowflakes whirling made a snowy, billowy gown, as beautiful as the girl who wore it in 1873, when Lady Rose went to make her curtsy to the Queen.

1873

Rose's dress was of white chiffon, not more snowy than her pretty white shoulders rising from it, and looped up with lilies-of-the-valley and white heather in posies. And that morning Papa had clasped a string of pearls round her throat and slipped a pearl bracelet on either wrist, and Mamma had added a silver filigree butterfly to clip in her hair, with seed pearls scattered like dewdrops on its wings. She had white satin slippers and long white gloves, and a real lace handkerchief to carry in her white brocade bag; and because it was May and very warm her cloak was of white satin lined with pink chiffon, and had the neatest swansdown collar that fastened with a silver thistle-brooch under her chin. She looked lovely, and her cheeks were glowing; tears of excitement kept glittering on her eyelashes and she dared not brush them off for fear of marking her gloves. White kid marked so easily.

Rose, Ann Dalrymple, Susan Jardine, and their chaperon were packed into the carriage; every inch of space in that carriage foamed with their billowing dresses.

Ann, who had been brought up in genteel seclusion on her father's Lowland estates, had never even seen the Queen, and had been so impressed by her Mamma with the awesome dignity and glory of Royal Majesty that she was almost prepared to fall flat on her face when the Vision should be revealed.

The carriage was drawn up now before the great, grey palace under its frowning mountain barrier; and there was red carpet on the steps, and an awning, and powdered footmen gorgeously adorned and accoutred coming forward to open the door.

" I'm *so* excited," murmured Susan Jardine; " and my dress is *so* tight. Seventeen inches at the waist, Rose. Mamma was nearly bursting with pride, and I was holding my breath. Bother! I've broken another rosebud off its stalk. I shan't have anything but stalks by the time I get to the Presence."

Rose giggled. " There's Lady Leithern, and Lady McIntyre. What does she remind you of in that very shiny black plush?"

" A seal. A *trained* seal."

" Oh, please, Susan! Don't make me laugh."

The three girls, remembering their instructions, became intensely solemn and awed as they were shepherded up the great staircase, and into the drawing-room where débutantes and chaperons were waiting. It was a magnificent

88

WHEN LADY ROSE WENT TO MAKE HER CURTSY TO THE QUEEN

room, glittering with light from the huge crystal chandeliers, and gay with the high laughter and chiming voices of girls.

"The chairs," explained Rose, "were all worked in tapestry by the ladies of Scotland. I remember Mamma's in red and white and gold. I wish I could see it now. I believe the Duchess of Blair is sitting on it."

"I could ask her to get up," suggested the irrepressible Susan. "She's my great-aunt."

"Oh, don't do that!" cried Ann, taking her seriously and growing pale at the contemplation of any misdemeanour. "Rose, do you think Queen Mary used to use this room?"

"Oh, no," said Rose. "Her rooms were right away over at the other side of the Palace, in the north-west tower. And there is the old banqueting hall where Prince Charlie gave his ball; I don't suppose you'll see that to-day. These are the modern apartments."

"Where is the Throne Room?"

"Just through that door. We shall be going in a minute."

The heralds were sounding their silver trumpets; the doors were flung wide; the crystal, dancing lights beat down on the portraits of the Royal Family with which the walls of the Throne Room were hung: on the assembly of Scottish nobility; on coronets and tiaras, diamonds and rubies and sapphires, on golden and auburn and raven-black heads, on satin and velvet and silk and gauze, and banks of flowers, and glittering uniforms and liveries and swords and flags and emblems. Victoria, Queen of Scotland, was about to hold her Court.

The whole assembly had sunk to the ground on bended knee and in billowing curtsy; there was a clash of swords; the band was playing *God Save the Queen*, and following after came the wild blood-stirring welcome of the pipes.

Rose raised her eyes, and saw the little regal black-clad lady, her breast a-gleam with Orders and Stars, her throat and wrists blazing with the jewels of the Realm, and behind her throne the Duke of Connaught and the Duke of Argyll and the Royal ladies. Rose's heart was bursting with excitement; her eyes were dazzled; a sob of ecstasy rose in her throat. At the sight of the Scots lords, her father's friends, in the glory of the Scottish dress, the kilt, the velvet coat, the lace at throat and wrist, she was so thrilled and elated that she forgot her first shyness; her satin-shod foot was even tapping softly to the skirl of the pipes.

"How the Queen must love it!" she was thinking. "How she must burn with joy at being in Scotland. Nothing they could show in England could be so beautiful and so grand as this."

She caught sight of her parents and was warm with pride. Papa looked magnificent with his purple velvet coat and flowing laces and silver sword, and Mamma was as lovely as a dream in blue-and-silver taffetas and all her jewels.

She vaguely heard Ann's whisper, " I'm terrified, but *isn't* it glorious?" and saw eager Susan blushing at the glances of a Highland officer; then they were gone before her, and it was Rose's turn, and she sailed forward as though floating on air, with glowing cheeks and brilliant eyes, and sank down in an exquisite curtsy before her Majesty, her ears full of music and her breath with perfume.

" Who is the girl?" they were asking.

" Lady Rose Targenet, Lochlule's girl."

" She's very striking. She has a manner."

" Rather too much so for eighteen, don't you think? A little too confident? I like to see a girl timid and hesitating like the little Dalrymple."

" Lady Rose is the Keepsfield heiress."

" She has the air of being somebody's heiress. I wouldn't call her beautiful."

" *Mais non. Spirituelle, je pense.*"

" That is a word I don't trust. She looks to have a mind of her own; a pity, in a girl."

Rose wouldn't have cared what they said about her. It

was all over, and she had loved it and seen the most brilliant sight that the flower of Scotland had to offer; and now they were in the withdrawing-room again and someone had given her a glass of champagne—the first in her life—and the most divine little sandwiches, of which etiquette forbade her to take more than two, though her eyes followed the salver longingly.

" I don't know what's in them," she told Susan; " only we never have it at home."

" Perhaps it is paté of peacock," suggested Susan.

" Oh! Why?"

" Because it sounds the kind of food they would eat in the palace."

" Did you like the presentation?" whispered Ann. " Was I all right? Did my ankles show? Mamma said she'd send me back to school for a year if my ankles showed when I made my curtsy."

" They didn't show," said Rose. " You looked very nice. I heard someone say so."

" Oh, what a relief. Rose!"

" Yes."

" Do you think we could see the picture of Prince Charlie?"

" I'll ask a footman."

" Oh, dare you?"

" Of course. Don't be silly."

93

The footman was most obliging, and led the way to a small room where the three girls found themselves alone.

"There, ladies!"

They stood in a row, with linked arms, three pretty Scottish girls in their exquisite dresses, two fair heads and one brown, gazing up at the beautiful picture. A young, golden prince in a green velvet suit, with lace at his throat and a slim sword at his side, almost stepping out of the frame to greet them, all the sunlight that the artist's brush could capture falling on his bright face and form.

"He's so beautiful," said Susan. "Why isn't there anybody like him alive to-day?"

"There may be," suggested Rose hopefully. "We haven't seen many young men."

"If there were," said Ann, "he might not fall in love with you, Susan."

"I think *he* spoils you for other men," said Rose dreamily. "I'm awfully in love with him."

"So am I," agreed Susan.

"I think *dark* men are very romantic," said Ann.

"Girls! What are you doing?" It was Lady Dunblane come in search of them.

"We're looking at Prince Charlie," explained Susan.

Lady Dunblane smiled. "Don't let that artist put ideas into your heads. I don't suppose Charles Edward was half

so handsome as he is painted.   At eighteen it is very easy
to fall in love with a picture."

"I wish I were Queen Victoria," breathed Rose, "and
then that picture would belong to me."

Susan began to chuckle.   "Some day, perhaps, you
might save the Queen's life, and she might say, 'Ask what
you desire, Lady Rose, to the half of my kingdom'; and
you would say, 'Ma'am, I crave a boon.   The portrait of
Prince Charles that hangs in your Majesty's withdrawing-
room at the Palace of Holyroodhouse.'"

"You couldn't have it even then," observed practical
Ann; "because I expect it belongs to the nation."

"Come," said Lady Dunblane.   "We are going now."

"But there's still the dance to-night!"

"Oh, yes.   You girls will adore the dance."

It was a Scottish ball to be held at the Edinburgh
Assembly Rooms.

Anyone who has ever been to a Scottish ball in Edinburgh knows that it is one of the most extravagantly
romantic and colourful functions in the world.   All the
men wore the kilt; all the women had shoulder-knots and
sashes of the tartan on their light frocks.   The pipes of the
Highland regiments played eightsome reels and country
dances, and the long lines of dancers went swaying, tripping, with tapping feet over the shining floor, brilliant
under the candlelight.

Rose had danced the reels until she was almost breathless; her face was radiant, she had never looked so pretty. Her heart was borne up, up, with the music of the pipes; her spirits responded to the gay and magic air, here in the ballroom, and outside where city and castle, rock and wynd, lay dark under the yellow stars. What a lovely world to be in; to be young and beginning life in a wonderful city on a night of May. Her fingers flew to refasten the brooch which held the knot of ribbons on her shoulder, her mother's family tartan.

Her mother was coming now, bringing a young man, just a rather pleasant, ordinary, serious-eyed young man. Rose smiled with a flash of regular white teeth. She was so happy she would have smiled at the whole world.

" Mr. Duncan of Kirkobothy, Rose; my daughter, Mr. Duncan. He wishes to dance with you."

" Oh, a waltz!" cried Rose. "How lovely!" Mr. Duncan bowed. " I enjoy the waltz too."

She slipped into the circle of his arm and he whirled her out upon the floor. She surrendered; she floated on air on an ecstasy of motion. She thought enjoyment could not be more complete; but the music! What were the strings playing? The loveliest melody adapted to waltz-time; the loveliest of songs, " Over the sea to Skye."

" Oh, listen!" whispered Rose, her eyes flashing with joy. " Oh, Mr. Duncan! ' Over the sea to Skye.' "

"I know. Isn't it delicious?"

Round and round, whirling and weaving, in that spin-
ning radiant throng, unconscious of the weight of your
body, forgetful of your flying feet, like a bird wheeling
over the sparkling sea . . . "Fly, bonny boat, like a bird
on the wing . . . Onward! the sailors cry . . . Carry the lad
that was born to be king . . . Over the sea to Skye!" It
was the most beautiful thing, Rose thought, that had ever
happened; she would remember it as long as she lived. On
and on went the music; on and on the dance . . . "Carry
the lad that was born to be king " . . . In all her wildest
dreams Rose had never thought of anything so ecstatic as
this . . . "Over the sea to Skye." Words and melody
alike, to stir the heart.

It was over, and the echoes of the music were dying
away. Rose smiled at her partner.

"That was exciting. How well you dance! But I think
it was the music. It seemed to carry us."

"On the wings of song?"

"Yes, that was it. This is the first dance I've ever been
to; you are my first real partner."

He smiled too; he was older than she had thought at
first, about thirty-five. She couldn't be embarrassed with
anyone so old as that, nearer the generation of her father,
she thought.

"Shall we sit down, Lady Rose? Where is your fan?"

"I can't imagine. I must have lost it, but it doesn't matter. The dance was worth it. Oh, that song! I think it is the loveliest tune in the world, 'Fly, bonny boat, like a bird on the wing!'" . . . She hummed, and laughed, her eyes blue and clear as summer waters.

"You like the Scots ballads?"

"Yes, only they usually make me cry."

"Why?"

"*Why?* You a Scot, Mr. Duncan, and you ask me why!"

"It was a shame," he admitted; "but I wanted to hear it put into your own words. You're different from most young girls, Lady Rose."

Her eyes widened apprehensively.

"How? What do you mean? Do you mean—people won't like me?"

"Just the opposite. You have sensibility."

"I want people to like me."

"You were only presented to-day?"

"Yes. I'm just beginning to live. I've been at school in England; it was dreadful. Where do you live, Mr. Duncan?"

"At Kirkobothy House near Invercaldy."

"Oh, what a long way away. I shall probably never see you again."

He laughed lightly; his eyes, Rose thought, were kind.
"That sounds portentous, Lady Rose. Are you propos-
ing to leave the country?"

"Leave the country? Leave Scotland? Heavens, no!
Never! Never as long as I live."

"That's a rash thing to say."

"But nothing could tempt me, and now I'm grown up
and can choose for myself nothing can make me."

"And now you are grown up, and are going to stay
in Scotland for ever, what do you propose to do with your
life?"

Rose cupped her chin on her hand and looked thoughtful. "I don't quite know. I shall stay at Keepsfield, of
course; and now I'm entitled to go to Court I shall go
every year. But I should like to do something very noble
as well; I should like to go down to history."

"There's nothing like having ambition," said Duncan
quizzically. "I think it is mostly the men who go down
to history."

Rose lifted saddened eyes. "I know. The famous women
generally die, like the Martyr of Solway Firth. I'd hate
to die, just to be in history. But I'm only eighteen; I'm
sure to find something to do. I think things develop more
when you get older."

"They certainly do!"

"Is it very beautiful where you live, Mr. Duncan?"

"Very. You should see our deer forests and our mountains. My house is at the head of the loch. The water is always a brilliant green, as though it were distilled from emeralds, except in autumn, when it turns gold like the bracken on the slopes above. My servants speak the Gaelic. The house is only small, but it is old and belongs to my family. I love it dearly."

"That is the way I feel about Keepsfield, only Keepsfield is rather large. I have a *little* picture of it that an artist made; I took that to England to school."

"Shall we dance again? The music is beginning."

Her eyes danced. "An eightsome? Oh, yes!"

When the dance was over Rose caught her mother's warning eye. She said regretfully, "I must go. Goodbye, and thank you for that lovely waltz. I shall remember it as long as I live."

"Won't you come outside and see how exquisite a May night can look in Edinburgh?"

"I mustn't. Mamma keeps beckoning."

He pressed her fingers. "I hope you'll be happy, Lady Rose, and do all the things you want to do."

She gave a sigh of pure pleasure. "Oh, I shall. Being grown up is so perfect."

Mamma was angry. "You danced twice with that man, Rose, and sat with him for at least ten minutes. It was indiscreet. Do realize, my darling child, that your whole social future depends on the impression you make at the beginning. People are watching you."

"Yes, Mamma."

She sat demurely enough on the gilt chair at her mother's side, content to watch the dancing, the girls, the men, the swing of the kilt and flutter of a tartan sash; to hear the tap of buckled shoes and the light swish of gliding feet, the laughter, and the Scottish airs, and the soul-thrilling clamour of the pipes. Behind her a velvet curtain covered a long window; she drew it back cautiously and peeped out. It was the most perfect night. Edinburgh lay hushed in the soft moonlight and the air was windless and warm. Rose could smell the scent of a peat fire from somewhere among those old clustered houses. Black against the silvery sky climbed the Castle Rock, the battlements, and the sharp, fantastic silhouette of the roofs of the Royal Mile. It was like an illustration from a fairy-tale. Life was rather like a fairy-tale altogether. She dropped the curtain abruptly.

"Rose, Lady Dunblane is speaking to you."

"Yes, Mamma. Thank you, Lady Dunblane, for chaperoning me this afternoon."

"And have you enjoyed your day, my dear?"

"*Enjoyed it!* There aren't any words to say what a beautiful day I've had."

"She will learn to be more restrained," said the

Countess. " Enthusiasm is so tiring, Rose, and I'm *afraid*
it may give you wrinkles. You may dance again if you
wish. Sir James MacKenzie is coming your way; and
come back here to me the *minute* the music ceases."

Rose sat up in bed next morning and read a long, long
account of her début in the *Edinburgh Gazette*. Her dress
was accurately described, and she thoughtfully " tasted "
the adjectives they had assigned to her. " Sprightly ", she
decided, was a hideous word. It interested her to learn
what had never occurred to her before, that she was the
most important Scottish débutante of the year. Among
her notes was a little packet containing white heather from
her partner, Duncan of Kirkobothy. The spray slipped
from her fingers on to the satin coverlet; her eyes grew
thoughtful. Important? *She* was important? She, Rose
Targenet, aged eighteen, who had done so little but rejoice
in the beauty and happiness of life. Of course her importance was not her own quality; it was because of Papa.
Importance wasn't the same as greatness either; other
circumstances—like having the Earl of Lochlule for your
Papa—could make you important, but you had to make
yourself great; and you had to *be* great, in your heart, and
do great things. You might even have to die for your
country, but when the time came you didn't shrink. It
wasn't enough just to enjoy the brilliance and bloom of
the Realm of Scotland—like yesterday; you had to be ready

for the strife and the dust, and the cold, harsh wind of Duty. Prince Charlie's men could dance in velvet coats at Holyrood; but they could also die in the rain at Culloden.

She breathed suddenly, " Oh, God, please make me great! "—and then held her breath, fearful at the thought of her impulsive prayer.

She slipped out of bed, and saw that the sun was sparkling on Princes' Gardens; there was a most inviting scent of spring in the air. She began to dress quickly, eager to be out. The spray of white heather, forgotten, tossed among the covers of the bed, was discovered by a housemaid, laid in a drawer, and never remembered again.

7

Nay, to earth's life in mine some prescience, or dream, or desire
(How shall I name it aright?) comes for a moment and goes—
Rapture of life ineffable, perfect—as if in the brier,
Leafless there by my door, trembled a sense of the rose.

WILLIAM DEAN HOWELLS

CHAPTER V

HELEN DACRE had been brought up in a north of England industrial city. Her father was a hardworking doctor; one of those devoted, shabby men who all day long dash from door to door, from poorly furnished bedroom to overcrowded kitchen, dealing with influenza epidemics, and outbreaks of measles, and rickety babies, and asthmatic old people; sometimes paid, sometimes unpaid, working for love not money. From childhood Helen, accepting crowding and discomfort for her body, had demanded the best for her mind. She was by nature a student. She attended the University in her home city, and there mingled with the most intelligent and progressive set. It was among them that she met her husband. She was austere in her tastes, passionately loved beauty, but never desired luxury. She always had the kind of spirit that could lift her above her surroundings; not that she was " other-worldly ", for she would cheerfully occupy herself with the affairs of the big, dark, inconvenient house to relieve her mother, but her pleasures were intellectual and gave her infinite joy. The friends of her youth were all students and young people of purposeful and intelligent mind. After her marriage she and her husband chose their intimates from among people who worked hard and had more brains than money. Her knowledge of a world outside her own was drawn merely from books; therefore her first glimpse of such a world, at Keepsfield, made her feel as though she were weaving the fabric of a dream. Now in that dream one figure was coming to life, the figure of Lady Rose. She was no creation of the mind; she had really lived and felt. She had *belonged*—this was an awesome thought—to all this rich beauty as young Helen Candless had belonged to the soot-blackened house in the Liverpool street. And as the Liverpool house now looked in vain for the escaped Helen, so did glorious Keepsfield for its vanished Lady Rose.

Now Mrs. Dacre had broken the ice with the old caretaker she felt she could really talk.

" You are making her live for me," she said sympathetically. " I mean, your Lady Rose."

The old woman looked with surprise.

" Do you feel that, madam? I wonder why. I've said so little about her."

" Then it must be the way you've said it. I'm picturing her now in all these vast rooms, on these terraces, in the gardens. I was at Holyroodhouse the other day, and they took us round the royal apartments. We had to pay six-pence for we were just tourists, not what my husband called ' presentable ' people. That's a joke! But we saw the Throne Room, and the thrones and the royal portraits, and I pictured the scene at Court with all the colour and the uniforms and the pretty girls, and the kilts and pipers. And now I can see Lady Rose in that very room, as she must have been. Did you see her in that dress?"

" Oh, yes, madam; I remember it well."

" Don't take any notice of the men," said Helen. " Please sit down and talk to me. You love this place, don't you?"

A spasm passed over the old woman's face, but she gave a quick smile.

" You see, madam, I loved it when I was a tiny child."

" I know. *Really* I understand, though my life has been very different and far away from anything like this. Please, Mrs. Memmary, could you tell me some more about Lady Rose?"

" What do you want to know?"

" Just how her happy life went on. I can't leave her now. There she is, with her bright face and her lovely frocks, setting out to be a young lady. Did she have what they call a wonderful season? Did people adore her? Did she—well, I shouldn't ask, but I should so much like to know if she had a lover. It isn't just idle curiosity; it's the magic of the day and of this place. She must have left the imprint of her personality; I feel her near."

The old woman's blue eyes were bent on her thin, work-knotted hands.

"I could tell you if you want to know. It's warm here in the sun. Lady Rose wasn't here very much that summer she was presented. They took her away to London for the season; and when she came back she was engaged to be married. That was the proper thing, of course."

"Engaged!" Helen made a slight gesture of the hand. "But begin where she went to London, please. How did it all happen?"

"I can only tell you what I saw and heard," said the caretaker.

She wrinkled her old brow, trying to recapture that vanished day. Helen waited at her side.

1873

Lady Rose thought a great deal about marriage. All girls of eighteen do, especially when, like Rose, they are having their first season in society and meeting a great many young women who think about nothing else. First you were presented, and then you acquired quantities of new clothes, and then you went to London, and it was all balls and operas and, above all, match-making. Sooner or later you would have to " make a match ". Everybody did. And one of two things happened; either your family were simply delighted because you had made a " good match ", or else they became rather quiet and subdued and tried to hush up the fact that you had made a " poor match ". All the girls had giggled over a parodied rhyme . . .

> In the Spring manœuvring mothers whisper in the stern aside,
> He is but the second brother; you must never be his bride.

However, quite apart from the quality of the match— (for according to the whim of fate you might become the fiancée of a marquis like little Agatha Melling who wasn't even pretty; or you might make the best of a penniless but handsome guardsman like the eldest Blandshire girl)—in the end you married and your whole life was changed.

Rose indulged in the most romantic dreams about marriage. Of course they were all delightfully vague and abstract, and for all practical purposes they began and ended with white satin and pearls and sheaves of flowers at St. George's, and red carpet in front of Aunt Violet's house in Belgrave Square, and tears, and hundreds of presents. After that came a kind of ideal and undefined state in which you lived blissfully under a new name, and had your own carriage, and didn't have to ask permission from

Mamma when you wanted to go out. Floating airily through all this, of course, was a man. He was not like any man you had ever seen; *they* were just men. This man—your husband, queer, mysterious word—was hardly human at all. He was dreadfully handsome, and a little frightening, but of course you didn't see very much of him. When you did see him there were love scenes. He always called you " my darling " in a deep, tender voice; and he gave you jewels and flowers, and sometimes went down on his bended knees to kiss your hand. All this came out of the books you had read. Some day, almost any time after you were presented and began to go about with Mamma, you would suddenly meet this marvellous being. You would be in love. You would be married. And that was the end, except that, of course, you would live happily ever after.

" I know what he will be like," said Rose to her friend, Hermione Southwood, as they were dressing for the opera. " He will be exactly like the picture of Bonnie Prince Charlie at Holyrood; all golden and smiling and stepping out of the frame to meet you."

" Will he be in Highland dress? " asked Hermione, whose imagination was limited, and who was inclined to take Rose literally.

" Not necessarily," said Rose. " Of course he must be Scots. But if I saw him for the first time in the kilt, I really think, Hermione, I should die with excitement. He'd be *too* beautiful. But I know he's golden and blue-eyed and like a god. What is yours like?"

"I'd rather have a dark man," said Hermione thoughtfully. "Rather pale, you know, and with a beautiful, glossy, black moustache, like Mr. Darcy in *Pride and Prejudice*. I couldn't bear anybody fat; could you, Rose?"

"Oh, no!" Rose shuddered. "Or old. Or bald."

It was June, and she was staying with her aunt, the Duchess of Shyre, in Belgrave Square. She was fascinated by this, her first grown-up visit to London. It was so different from Edinburgh; so much more glittering and sophisticated and varied, and there were such crowds of people and so many places where you had to be seen. There was a little balcony at the back of her mother's small third-floor sitting-room in the Belgrave Square house, and here Rose would sometimes crouch on a cushion looking out over the roofs and spires of the city, washed golden by the sparkling London sunshine.

One afternoon they had been to a tiring garden-party, and when they reached home Rose was glad to slip off her tight shoes and gloves, and heavy flower-laden hat. She ran to the little balcony, made a pile of cushions, and sat down with her hands clasped round her knees. Her head sank back drowsily. She slept. She woke to the sound of voices through the open french window. Conversation between her mother and her aunt came to her clearly. With horror she realized that she had already heard too much to reveal herself. They could not see her. If only they would go away so that she could escape! But they went on talking, and Rose made the best of a bad situation and was bound to admit that she found the conversation almost too interesting.

"You will have to watch Rose very shrewdly," the Duchess was saying. "She's the incalculable type. When it comes to making a match she might do anything."

"Oh, but I've brought Rose up so carefully," said Lady Lochlule. "I'm sure I can rely on her intelligence and wisdom. Rose has never been in the least wilful or independent."

"I know all that," said the Duchess; "but I understand girls. I've had four of my own and all well married. Three of them were sensible girls, and the fourth was all up in the clouds, like Rose."

"Really, Janet, Rose is most sensible."

"In many ways, yes, Margaret. I'm quite sure that Rose is a good daughter, but she has far too much imagination, and these imaginative girls do the most unexpected and disconcerting things. Look at Alix Caithness's girl. Just like Rose, all poetry and ideals, and married a rector's son—a penniless barrister of no family at all. Of course I know he's done well and made a lot of money, but he mightn't have done so; and that girl could have been Viscountess

Melrock! Really, with these toothy Americans competing now, it makes one's blood boil to see our own girls not making the best use of their chances. Rose reads novels; I should stop her. And Alfred Tennyson's poetry which is even worse! If poor Alfred must write about what he calls love, he might at least explain that it is an emotion to be openly enjoyed only by the middle classes. Have you spoken to Rose about a match?"

"Not directly. I don't believe in that. When the time comes Rose will be guided by her Papa and myself. I don't contemplate any difficulty."

"Rose must be made to realize the responsibility of her position."

"Oh, I think she does. You see, having no heir——"

"Very unfortunate, Margaret," said the Duchess drily. "I hope that wasn't your fault! However, there it is. Rose is her father's heiress. Have you ever mentioned the matter to the Queen?"

"The Queen mentioned it to me. She was in a very good humour and had been rather attracted by Rose at the drawing-room. She said that all being well, Rose would become a peeress in her own right. Countess of Lochlule."

"Then it matters tremendously whom she marries!"

"Really, Janet, do you think I don't know it? I hope you are not going to tell me that you have noticed Rose dancing with anyone undesirable?"

"She danced with Pontathol's younger boy last night, but she didn't seem interested. In any case, even a younger Pontathol wouldn't be too bad. Rose will have the title; so family matters most, and the Pontathol blood is pure. No actresses or Yankees!"

"We have thought," said the Countess, "that if we could link up the Keepsfield estate——"

"Oh? Have you actually got eligibles adjoining?"

"Hush. I really wouldn't care to put this into words, Janet, but there *is* just a possibility."

"Do tell me!"

"I mustn't. Really I mustn't. But if anything comes of it, you shall be the first to know."

"Money, of course?"

"Oh, yes."

"And the family?"

"Oh, very, very well connected on both sides. His mother is a Lauchlane, and his father's mother was a Gordon. He's only a baronet, but its an old Scottish title, and he has ten thousand acres practically adjoining Keepsfield."

"My dear Margaret."

"Oh, I shouldn't have said so much, I really shouldn't."

"Is he in London now?"

"He will be next week. He's staying with the Gourlays."

"But so is the Prince of Wales."

"I know. They are quite friendly. Janet, not a word!"

"Tell me. Is Rose prepared?"

"She hasn't even met him. But what does it matter? She'll be carried off her feet; girls of eighteen always are. That is why I think it so important that they shouldn't drag on into a second and third season. After a girl has had three seasons her parents haven't the slightest control over her. Look at Lady Boswell's girl! Scandalous! And twenty-three already; practically on the shelf."

"Well, Margaret, I'm very, very interested. Nothing could give me greater pleasure than to see Rose well married. If you wish the wedding in London you can have this house."

"Janet! You must not rush on so! It is positively indelicate of you."

"Take my advice," said the Duchess, "and stop the girl from reading novels. Girls of eighteen have no business to read love scenes in print; it puts false ideas into their heads. Operas at Covent Garden are bad enough, heaven knows, with persons actually romantically embracing each other on the stage. But I hastened to impress on Rose and Hermione Southwood that it all happened hundreds of years ago, and that in any case it is extremely doubtful whether Dido and Aeneas actually existed. I myself will lock Tennyson in my bureau; and if you see Rose reading any other poetry

I do implore you, Margaret, for your own sake, to substitute something wholesome. A young girl needs to read nothing but her Bible; and only carefully selected portions of that!"

"We must go and dress," said the Countess. "Dinner is early on account of the ball. What a chaperon has to endure!"

"I had four daughters to chaperon," said the Duchess. "I yawned my way through six seasons for those girls, but it was worth it. They did me credit; even Frances, who was as romantic as Rose herself. You can't help it; girls like that need guiding, and marriage with the right man will soon take the romance out of them."

The two ladies left the room, and a moment later Rose escaped to her own apartment. She was so excited that she could hardly be patient with her maid. It was all new and thrilling, and though some of her aunt's remarks had sounded rather sinister, the dazzling fact emerged that she was going to make a brilliant match. She was probably going to be married to somebody who lived near Keepsfield. Who could he be? What would he be like? He knew the Prince of Wales. Would he wear the kilt? For he was Scots, thank goodness. She would have a wedding and wear satin and pearls and lilies. What did the Duchess know about love and romance? What could any person over thirty know about romance in any case! Tristram and

Iseult, the Shakespearian lovers, and those strangely thrilling people of whom she had read secretly not long ago in a forbidden book called *Wuthering Heights*—Heathcliff and Catherine Linton . . . Her heart quickened; her blood ran hot under her throbbing pulses. "And they are gone; aye, ages long ago these lovers fled away into the storm . . ." To-night, and all the nights now, she would dream of her unknown lover!

The season ran on. Balls, garden-parties, a wedding; balls, Ascot, another wedding, Goodwood, luncheon with the Queen at Windsor, bridesmaid at the biggest wedding of all. Lovely frocks and hats, and exciting food, and sometimes a glass of champagne, and flowers for her hair, and compliments, and waltz tunes—but none so lovely as those the pipers played in Edinburgh town. Rose was excited and happy; life was so beautiful. Chaperons were looking tired but triumphant. Lady Chingfield had successfully disposed of no less than three daughters; mothers galore in grey lace and pearls had fluttered blissfully into the front pews of St. George's and St. Margaret's. Rose had been one of twelve bridesmaids when the Duchess of Wend's daughter had married Prince Henri of Toulouse. Hermione Southwood and Ann Dalrymple were both engaged. Hyde Park was looking a little tarnished; the heavy trees were dusty; the roses crumbled and paled in the borders.

Everybody was going North; and—oh, joy of joys—Rose

was going back to Keepsfield again. It was August, and royal Scotland was putting on purple robes and burnishing her crown of mountain-tops. Rose was hungry for the tang of the heather and the salt wind blowing over the Firth of Forth, and the kingdom of Fife and the sight of the emerald border of East Lothian on the farther shore.

1874

There was to be a large house-party at Keepsfield. Now was the noble house to show forth all its glory; the dignity of powdered footmen and marble glimmering halls, and crystal chandeliers beyond the power of three men to lift. The covers came off the chairs in the pink drawing-room; chairs of palest pink satin worked by hand in intricate patterns of silver thread and blue silk. Bedrooms were prepared with new and lavish canopies and coverlets and hangings of satin and velvet and brocade. The priceless old furniture was polished till it gleamed like dark satin. The great table in the dining-hall was extended to seat sixty people; and footmen staggered about under the weight of the massive, ornamented silver services which had been the envy of George the Fourth when he visited his Scottish earls. The serried rows of life-sized ancestors in oils gazed out across the wide park where once they had ruled. Forty gardeners were at work in the park and gardens. The cellars were full of priceless wines and fabulous quantities of food. Tapestries worked by the ladies of Lochlule when the old castle stood on the sight of the present house, came forth from their careful seclusion and hung on the walls of broad, panelled corridors. Furniture and pictures, ivory and china, statues and golden trinkets of priceless cost were set about the spacious rooms. A crystal fountain played in the hall and the scented water ran away through the mouths of golden dolphins. Painted ceilings and panelled galleries gleamed remote and vast. The state rooms where kings had slept were prepared as for royalty; the small drawing-room in this suite—a room thirty feet long—was a vision of white and gold and smelt of lilies. The bedroom was lilac and purple, and the hangings and bed-covers were stiff with pearls and gold. Carpets everywhere were—apart from their vastness—treasures beyond price from Persia and China. All the great rooms were filled with flowers; and the tall, unveiled windows shone out on brilliant vistas of garden and park and forest. The Countess's jewels came up in all their magnificence from the strong room. There were tremendous and unceasing preparations below stairs, for there were to be forty guests and they would bring with them fifty or sixty personal servants. Everything was done with the lavish splendour that surrounds an income of £70,000 a year.

The reason for all this was an announcement which had appeared in the Engagements column of the London *Times* the last week in January, and had been given first place in that interesting column in recognition of the rank of those it celebrated.

> A marriage has been arranged and will shortly take place between Major Sir Hector Galowrie, K.C.M.G., Black Watch, of Redlace, Fife, and Lady Victoria Elspeth Rose Grahame-Rooth-Targenet, only daughter of the Earl and Countess of Lochlule.

Rose had ear-rings for the first time to wear at her engagement party, little roses made of pearls with diamond hearts, and her maid, Jean, was fastening them on. Rose tilted her head before the mirror; her eyes were blue and candid, and very, very bright.

" They're verra bonny, m'leddy," said Jean.

Rose laughed. " They make me look quite elderly. I suppose I ought to look elderly now I'm going to be married."

The mirror reflected a rather pale face, with merry lips a little more serious than usual, and blue eyes wide and critical under the coronet of glossy brown hair. The dress was of coffee-coloured tulle with big puffed sleeves and knots of scarlet velvet ribbon on the shoulders.

Rose suddenly caught sight of Jean's woe-begone expression.

"What's the matter, Jean? Don't you like the way I look?"

"Oh, m'leddy, you look beautiful. But——" Jean gave a little wail. "I couldn't help thinking you might not be wanting a country girl like me for your maid, when you get mairrit on such a fine gentleman as Sir Hector Galowrie."

"And why on earth not?"

"A French maid wad be cleverer at the hairdressing," Jean mumbled.

Rose made an impatient gesture. "Oh, you silly girl. As if I'd let you go, Jean! I'm used to you; I hope you'll always stay with me, you and all the other servants who have looked after me. I couldn't be happy with strange ones."

"The others? Oh! Can I tell them? They've been so anxious."

"Have they really? Give me just a flick more powder. I shall take them with me to Redlace. I want to have as much of Keepsfield about me as I can, even if I am married. Oh, Jean, I almost wish I weren't going away."

Jean's face broke into smiles. "Oh, but m'leddy, it isn't far; only six miles away to Redlace."

"I know. Isn't it lovely? Just what I should have chosen." Rose swung her mirror-stool round impulsively.

" Do you know, Jean, when there was so much talk of getting married I used to be frightened sometimes—yes, really frightened—that I might *have* to marry some one and go and live hundreds of miles away, like my friend Ann Dalrymple. I suppose I should have *had* to bear it. I've been lucky."

" Oh, you have!" cried Jean, clasping her hands. " And Sir Hector, isn't he the finest, handsome gentleman?"

" Yes, he's very handsome," said Rose. " Of course I always said I'd marry a fair man, but you can't *really* choose. I don't know Sir Hector *very* well; in fact, I'm a little bit frightened of him. Mamma says that is the right way to feel about one's future husband."

" He must be very much in love with you, m'leddy," said Jean. She was delighted to know that she was to remain in Lady Rose's service. The relationship between young mistress and young maid had always been very free and generous.

" He gives me a lot of presents," mused Rose, " though I don't think I care very much for family jewels. They're hard and icy-looking at the best of times. And at the worst, they're downright ugly."

" We're all very proud," said Jean, " that your leddyship has made such a fine match."

" Oh! Thank you!" said Rose, taken aback.

It was a fine match, and Rose knew it; though she felt

slightly oppressed at times. Magnificence was a definite check on high spirits; and her engagement seemed to have been the signal for letting loose a flood of magnificence upon her. Magnificence was suffocating; it consisted to Rose's way of thinking of new and stately relatives; gold plate, dignity, suppression of one's natural enthusiasms, and family heirlooms. However, she was assured by her Mamma that as an engaged young woman—and so suitably engaged too—she stepped upon a higher plane of conduct; and as a married woman, and the wife of a Galowrie, she would enter a realm of manners second only to that occupied by the Queen herself.

This was February, and the wedding was to be in Edinburgh in April. Presents were arriving. It was very exciting to open presents, though the contents were often disappointingly dull. Another salver; or Queen Anne salt cellars, or a heavy and grim black marble clock. The relatives came to the house-party.

"Come, Rose! So you've done very well for yourself after all!" said the outspoken Duchess of Shyre.

"Yes, Aunt. Thank you, Aunt," stammered Rose, wondering what exactly you did reply to that kind of remark.

Sir Hector's mother and sisters were formidable. The Dowager Lady Galowrie was said to have the stiffest back and the coldest eye in Scotland. She was once, by a graceless nephew, referred to as Blameless Bertha, because she had never been known to make a mistake. Her daughters were sandy-haired, sandy-skinned girls with large pale eyes, rather reminding one of a pair of goldfish. They all lived together in a very draughty house at Stirling, and made innumerable drab garments on their sewing machines for the strictly deserving poor.

There was a very charming Aunt Katy who came from an impoverished castle near Inverness. Everybody seemed to like her; though for some reason, obscure to Rose, they always referred to her as " poor Katy ". She fell in love with Rose at sight, and proved herself sympathetic.

" You've too much heart and too much imagination," she said to Rose one day when they were walking on the sand-dunes. " You're going to get hurt if you're not careful."

Rose looked surprised. " Hurt? How could I? I'm very happy."

" You're very young, my child."

" Has that got anything to do with it? "

" Oh, yes. You haven't been anywhere yet; you haven't lived. When you wake up and begin to live, that's when I'm afraid for you."

" When you're once married," said Rose, " nothing much else can happen to you, can it? "

" Oh, my God!" said Aunt Katy. " Can't it!"

Rose, who had never before heard a woman use strong language, was awed into silence.

" Will you live at Redlace?" asked Aunt Katy.

" Yes. I like the house—as much as I could like any house that wasn't Keepsfield."

" You're fond of country life? What do you do all the time?"

" Oh, entertain and speak French and sew and draw, and feed the animals and go walks."

" Ah, yes," said Aunt Katy. " One might have known. What a waste!" She added briskly, " I dare say you'll be all right. You're used to discreet seclusion. And of course you'll have to produce the heir, and a second string in case the heir breaks his neck, and a girl or two."

" Oh, yes," agreed Rose, whose knowledge of such matters was inconsiderable.

" I suppose you *do* want to marry my nephew Hector?"

" Yes, I do," said Rose again. " I have to get married; and he's a Scot and Redlace is so near, and everybody seems pleased and so am I."

" Too easily pleased, I shouldn't be surprised."

" What do you mean?" Rose asked. " And please will you tell me what can happen to you once you're married?"

" Not on my life!" said Aunt Katy. " Not on my very life. You're lovely, Rose, and I wish you very, very happy. If ever you get in trouble, come to me. Come straight to me. Promise that, and then forget everything else I've said."

Rose nodded. "You're kind. I like you. I promise, but I *don't* understand."

"Too much heart," muttered Aunt Katy as if to herself. "Bad. I'll see you through." (Alas! she died in rather poor circumstances before Rose's Archie was two years old.)

"Is it a bad thing," Rose asked breathlessly, battling against the wind that flaked the sand-dunes, "to have imagination?"

"Good," gasped Aunt Katy, gripping her muff. "A good thing. You enjoy everything so much more. It gives you so many worlds to live in; you skip lightly out of one into another. From star to star; comet-like."

"Then why did you say——"

"Because you suffer more. Double-edged sword."

"Like at Hampstead, when I nearly cried over Keats' hair."

"Did you do that? H'm. Worse than I thought. If you never suffer from anything more dire than literary sensibility you'll be lucky. Can you swim?"

"No," said Rose, rather bewildered by the abrupt change of subject.

"Shoot?"

"No. Papa would never let me try."

" All the better. My nephew Hector abominates sporting women. Once at dinner at my house I put him next
to Elizabeth Glocharnechty, who told him she had brought
down three stags and lifted a seventeen-pound salmon at
her brother's place the week before. Afterwards he said to
me that if I had any more female ghillies to bestow as
dinner partners I might reserve them for his uncle Archibald, who is deaf and practically blind. He was really
annoyed. He showed his good taste when he chose you.
I never had much to offer him; we're short of women at
Clairk. Perhaps he'll bring you to see me, but I'm not
sure. Nobody could call my house comfortable. It is barely
habitable; just a series of stone vaults. We sit with our
plaids round our necks in the winter, and all the dishes are
cold by the time they get to the dining-hall."

Rose laughed merrily. " We *must* come. I'd love it.
Have you a piper who plays round the table?"

" Did have," said Aunt Katy. " Not now. Can't afford
retainers. No bathroom either. Hector won't come. I've
got something you'd like. Prince Charlie's bonnet and
plaid."

Rose stood still, as though incredulity had checked her.

" You don't mean *really* his—that he *wore*?"

" Oh, yes. Quite genuine. Two of his hairs stuck
in the bonnet; brightish brown, not so gold as he's
painted."

"How wonderful! How perfectly *magic*. I'd give anything in the world to see them—just to touch them."

"You shall," said Aunt Katy curtly. "I'll make you happy. I'll give them to you for a wedding present."

"Oh!" said Rose. Her eyes filled with tears which the salt wind flicked away. "I can't believe it—I can't tell you—or thank you. Oh!"

"That's all right," said Aunt Katy, as though parting with her greatest treasure was a trivial matter. "They're in a glass case, with a lock and key. You can have the case, too."

"It's almost too wonderful to be true," said Rose. "You don't know how I thank you. I'd give up all the other presents for that."

"Including the Galowrie jewels, I suppose?"

"I don't like jewels very much," said Rose.

"H'm." Aunt Katy shook her head again. "You're a lovely young girl and less spoiled than I could believe it possible. For an heiress."

Rose was dancing against the wind, as she had danced when she was ten.

"Haven't asked her if she loves him," Aunt Katy was muttering to herself. "Won't, either. She doesn't know what love is. Hope to God she never will."

The men of the house-party—mostly relatives—were, Rose decided, easy to get on with. Men were divided into two classes: the intelligent kind, like Hector, her fiancé, and Duncan of Kirkobothy with whom she had danced at her presentation ball; and the heavy kind who paid compliments and adapted their conversation to you as though you were six years old.

Her Uncle Keith. "Well, well, well! So the Targenet lassie is grown up. Seems like yesterday she was so high. H'rm! H'rm! And what do you expect *me* to give you for a wedding present, Rose?"

"I don't know," said Rose, trying not to look exasperated and wondering whether she should disgrace herself by asking for six white horses and a box of Edinburgh rock. Sarcastic wit was an unpardonable error in well-brought-up young women.

"I don't know, Uncle," she said, demurely.

"She doesn't know! H'rm! H'rm! Is she easily pleased, I wonder; or does she think she'll get more by leaving it to her old uncle. Heh? Heh?"

"I don't mind," said Rose. "I—I don't want anything."

"Rubbish! I've got the very thing for you, my dear. Belonged to your aunt; been in the family a hundred years. It's a parure, diamonds and rubies. Very handsome ornament. You shall have it; it's yours."

"Oh! . . . Thank you, Uncle."

"Not at all, my dear. A woman of position ought to

have handsome jewels; something substantial like your
aunt used to wear. A diamond dog-collar that she couldn't
turn her head in, that's what I liked to see. None of your
piffling strings of pearls—bah! All right for simpering
young misses, but you're going to be the lady of Redlace,
Rose, as well as your father's heiress. Put my gift on when
you go to see the Queen. It's shone at Balmoral before to-
day. H'rm! H'rm!"

The only man who did not seem to possess this heavy
manner was Cousin Riall Murdoch. He was nearly forty,
dark, thin, silent, and a bachelor. At first Rose thought
him melancholy, but when she asked him about his home
he grew quite eloquent. He lived in a kind of hunting-
lodge near Achnasheen. He would stride up and down
the west terrace beside Rose telling about the glories of
the deer forests on Sgurr na Briarch and the wild caves
and the gushing rivers, the long chase and the arduous
climb, breaking at last into the Gaelic, striding along to the
crackle and rumble of uncouth speech, until Rose grew
excited and wished she too could speak this queer, savage
tongue, and rush away untrammelled to the mountains
and forests, hide in the Highland caves, bathe in the rivers,
follow the deer through the luscious heather under a broil-
ing sun—ah, but how mad! Cousin Riall Murdoch must
be slightly mad himself, and he was infecting her. Mamma
would be furious. Rose, reluctantly and from a sheer sense

of duty, began to drop Cousin Riall. She felt rather doubtful, too, about the propriety of owning such a relative when she saw his wedding present, which consisted of a collection of hunting-knives, fastened to a trophy which could be hung on the wall. The whole thing looked perfectly revolting, Rose thought, and she would even have preferred another gift of heavy jewellery; only her fiancé, Sir Hector, didn't seem to mind or find Riall's gift objectionable, which was the main thing.

Rose was growing to admire her fiancé tremendously. He was a fine figure of a man, as fine as Papa, and very handsome in a military way. His uniforms were magnificent. Of course Rose hardly ever saw him alone, because that was not considered *comme il faut* until they were married; but on the brief occasions when they did find themselves together she was able to be very interested in his medals and orders, and he was kind in explaining them to her. She and Mamma had driven over two or three times to Redlace, and Rose had seen the rooms which were to be hers. She was childishly delighted to find that there were green velvet curtains to her bed. She had always wanted velvet bed-curtains, and Mamma told her she was a ridiculous baby.

And then in the end she never went to live at Redlace at all. The wedding was to be in April, and it was within a fortnight of the day, when preparations were at their height, that the Earl of Lochlule developed a bad cold. Nobody thought very much of a mere cold in those days, and the Earl drank hot whisky and hoped for the best. In three days pneumonia was rending his lungs; and he noisily coughed his heart to a standstill one morning as dawn came bright and blowing to an April breeze over the sand-dunes.

The sudden horror of it temporarily paralysed the great house; but life must go on. The Earl's last whisper had been that the wedding should not be postponed on his account; so Rose, all in sombre grey and wearing a grey bonnet and veil, was married to a bridegroom with crape on his sleeve at St. Giles' Cathedral, Edinburgh, on the originally appointed day. There was no honeymoon; they returned to Keepsfield, and Mamma obligingly transferred herself to her own house at Doune.

A week later the Queen sent for Rose, and, accompanied by her husband, the new Lady Galowrie travelled to Windsor and was made Countess of Lochlule in her own right. Rose, owner of Keepsfield! Hers, all hers for ever! How happy she would be now because she wasn't ever going to Redlace; she wasn't going away at all, she had been given her heart's desire.

I do not hunger for a well-stored mind,
I only wish to live my life, and find
My heart in unison with all mankind.

EDMUND GOSSE

CHAPTER VI

I DON'T think Sir Hector ever quite forgave Queen
Victoria," said Mrs. Memmary.

"Forgave the Queen?" put in Helen Dacre quickly.
"Then what about his wife—Lady Rose, the new
Countess? Did he blame her?"

The old woman shook her head. "I think that must
have been at the bottom of it all. In those days men didn't
like their wives to have rights, or any standing, or position
of their own. And Sir Hector was very much of his period."

"Please tell me about it."

"About——?"

"They weren't happy; I know they were not. You're
telling me why: that Sir Hector always had a sense of
ranklement that his wife was Countess of Lochlule in her
own right."

"He never said so; he never showed it."

"That doesn't matter. If the feeling was there *she*
would be sensible of it."

Mrs. Dacre and the old caretaker were alone on the terrace. Fifty yards away across the lawn the two men were sitting on a felled stump, Van Elsen with hands clasped round his knee, pipe in mouth, and face uplifted to the sky, apparently day-dreaming; Dacre very busy with a sheet of paper and pencil trying to make some kind of a sketch.

It was easy to imagine that clocks had ceased ticking and that time was standing still; Helen Dacre resisted an impulse to look at her wrist-watch lest to be reminded of the hour should break her spell. Half closing her eyes she could see the air full of dancing gold specks; she made herself an elaborate fancy that these were all the seconds of all the minutes of all the hours, days, and years that sunshine had ever fallen on Keepsfield. Then she opened her eyes wide, and almost painfully took in the beauty of the scene that she might never, never forget it; the white majesty of façades and terraces, the green verdure of the lawns, the bowery banners of trees in the park, the lofty blue sky, the rolling white clouds, the suggestion of hills and sea not far away, colour-harmony that satisfied the artist in her. Out of the west, high up, went a flight of birds, etched on the silver-blue, and then the sun caught them and they flamed to gold and vanished. So at last from this stately place would she, Helen, go; and might there be some beauty in her going. The scent of roses, the scent of grass, and the scent of sparkling, sun-filled sea was blown, mingled, across the park, touched Helen's senses, and was gone. She had a sudden feeling that she dared not lift her eyes lest Lady Rose herself should be standing at an upper window, wondering at the intruder in such strange clothes. Not that Lady Rose would have minded; she would have been so kind.

Helen said suddenly, "You hear so much about unhappy marriages in these days, Mrs. Memmary; you didn't then. Women didn't expect to have very much, I suppose, except their board and lodging and their children. A little husbandly consideration was just an extra, but not to be counted upon; so you didn't complain if you didn't receive it. Now we expect *everything* in marriage, and if we don't get it we announce our dissatisfaction in no uncertain terms. I'm not surprised that Lady Rose—I mean the Countess—was unhappy. I didn't like the sound of Sir Hector from the first; I believe he turned out to be a domestic tyrant. I should like to hear that Lady Rose stood up to him; but, of course, she didn't, she was too adorably ' of her period '. Don't tell me that he was unkind to her and neglected her; not Lady Rose, I couldn't bear it!"

The old woman who had looked rather apprehensive and alarmed at the beginning of this speech, before the end seemed amused, in so far as she could be amused, that is to say, that her grave eyes and mouth relaxed a little.

"Oh, madam; no, indeed! Everyone thought them an

ideal couple. There was a great deal of entertaining at Keepsfield, and Sir Hector gave parties for his own friends at Redlace, and they went to Balmoral, and to Paris, and to Switzerland——"

"Then what was wrong? You practically told me that Lady Rose wasn't happy in her marriage."

"I'm afraid it was as you said, madam."

"I thought so! But to outward appearances——"

"Oh, to outward appearances everything was *ideal*. Of *course*." Mrs. Memmary looked shocked, and Helen realized that she naturally held the opinions of an older and stricter generation.

"In *our* day, madam," said Mrs. Memmary, "there was such a thing as *noblesse oblige*. People had respect for tradition. People of position would rather have died than reveal to the common public that there was anything wrong in their domestic relations. The way that titled people, even those of old families, to-day are not ashamed to appear in the divorce court is scandalous; it is the end of breeding and nobility. When I was young there were great ladies, to-day there are none."

"I'm afraid you are right," said Helen; "but go back to Lady Rose. The time is going, and I must know what happened to her. Did the years just go on, and on? How many of them before anything else happened to her? Oh, and tell me, *did* she have the heir? I can picture her with the most beautiful duck of a baby, and I hope he wasn't like his father."

The old woman knitted her brows, and her blue eyes were lowered.

"Oh, dear!" thought Helen. "I've offended her by speaking like that of a member of the family. She'll think me vulgar and rude."

But presumably that was not what Mrs. Memmary was thinking, for in a moment she raised her head and said quietly: "The Countess had three children. Archie the heir, who was called after his father, and Alastair, and little Mary-Jean."

1884
AUGUST

"Miss Susan Jardine, my lady."

"Susan!"

"Rose! Yes, it is I, after all these years. Nearly ten, I believe. I haven't even been in Edinburgh, so you can't blame me for not coming to see you. What a lovely, lovely place. You do seem to have everything in the world, don't you, Lady Lochlule? May I sit down?"

"Oh, Susan, do sit down, and don't be so absurd. If you knew how glad I am to see you! Do you remember when we were at school we used to say that when we married we'd visit one another every week?"

Susan made a grimace. "I remember. But here you are, superlatively married, and I'm not married at all. I'm a complete old maid. Rose, they couldn't—they simply couldn't—get anybody to marry me. My grandmother, who is absolutely frank, once told me why. She said, 'You're not pretty, you haven't any money, and you talk too much. The first keeps away the young men, the second the middle-aged men, and the third the old men; so you'll die a spinster, Susan, and you might as well resign yourself to it.' But there you are! I'm still talking too much, and I never meant to say all that. Tell me about yourself. I haven't long to stay."

Lady Rose pulled a chair close to her friend's. They were in her own sitting-room overlooking the lake.

"I've got three children. They're very amusing. Shall I send for them?"

"Oh, don't," said Susan, shaking out her plain cloth travelling dress and untying the strings of a green straw bonnet. "Don't. I'm terrified of children. I never know what to do with them. You can't scruff them up like puppies and admire their ears and teeth; and if you talk to them like intelligent human beings they only greet you with most disconcerting stares. I wanted to see you. You haven't altered very much."

"Neither have you, Susan. You look about fifteen."

"Your husband is famous, isn't he? I'm always reading

about him in the newspapers, in the Court news. Yes, I read the newspapers, and I ride astride. Why shouldn't I enjoy all the ' advanced ' things when I know that nobody will want to marry me in any case? Where is Sir Hector? Shall I see him?"

Lady Rose laughed. " He's at Redlace, his house, about six miles away. I could send someone for him."

" Oh, heavens; no, don't! I'd be terrified. Is he terrifying, Rose?"

Lady Rose nodded. " He is—rather."

" All husbands are. I know. My sisters never breathe until theirs are out of the house. Is he away a great deal?"

" Quite often. But where are you living now, Susan?"

" Oh, in England, at Manders Hall, in Derbyshire. That is partly what I came to tell you about. . . . May I look out of the window? What a glorious view! I should sit here a great deal, if I were you. But, no, I shouldn't; it would be too tantalizing. I should be off to find out exactly what it was like on the tops of those blue hills and what lay beyond."

" You wouldn't," said Rose, grimly. " Not if you were me. It would be exceedingly unsuitable conduct."

" Oh." Susan came slowly back to her chair. " Then there are drawbacks in being well married, too. Oh, Rose, isn't *any* woman free? Are we all prisoners?"

" What do you mean?"

" I mean, that we aren't expected to want to live, or to

do things, or achieve things. We haven't to have any
views or aspirations; and ideas are improper and dangerous.
You had all kinds of ' ideas ' if I remember rightly, but
you were clever enough to keep them in the background,
and so you made a good match, and you're married and
have three children, which I suppose is some sort of a fulfilment in life. But what have I got? Just a piece of needlework, and two disappointed, elderly minded parents, and
all the time in the world on my hands. If I had my way
women should be free to do the same things as men; come
and go as they wished, and read and talk, and be doctors
and lawyers, and financiers, and Members of Parliament,
and newspaper writers. Wouldn't that be wonderful?"

" It would. But it couldn't possibly happen."

" Only in Utopia. Oh, I do have such a wretched, dull
existence. Rose, is this huge, wonderful house all *yours*?
What wouldn't I do if I had a house of my own—a whole
house! Not just a poky bedroom which I mayn't even
decorate as I like. But whoever heard of a woman young
enough to have ideas owning a house of her own? The
trouble is I'm not sufficiently an old maid to have any
of the old maid's compensations. When I do get a house
I shall be so ancient and stuffy that all I shall think of is
fitting chintz petticoats to the chair legs and red flannel
sausages to the window-frames to keep the draughts off my
quaking bones. Horrible."

"What would you do if you had a house now?"

"Fill it with jolly people, and have a picnic all day every day, and talk nonsense, and lie on our backs in the hay, and sing very loud when we felt like it. Do you remember how we used to talk at St. Alma's about all the things we intended to do? Do you suppose one single girl has found it possible to do any of the things she wanted to do when she was at school?"

"I shouldn't think so," said Rose. "We always seem to be either driven or pushed. But how cheerful we are! Is this all you came to tell me? How pretty your bonnet is!"

"Yes," said Susan, with satisfaction. "It's absolutely the newest thing, well tilted forward and lots of hair showing. I don't know what on earth Mamma will say to it. I've been staying with Aunt Eva at St. Andrew's, and she had this put away in her cupboard. She'd bought it in London a fortnight ago—*straight* from Paris—and then decided it didn't suit her. Neither did it, poor soul. You know, Father's side of the family are all a bit equine, and the first time Auntie went out in this, she met a carriage-horse with *its* straw bonnet on and *its* ears sticking through. Everybody saw it at once, and Auntie was so embarrassed. So she gave me the bonnet, and I think it's adorable."

"You'll stay!" cried Rose, jumping to her feet. "I'll have a room got ready for you, a really pretty one. And you can do as you like all the time you're here; only, darling, do be rather careful when Hector's about, won't you? You needn't bother about luggage, because I can give you everything——"

"Oh, Rose! Don't tempt me so. I can't stop. I'll tell you why in a minute. It was only by the sheerest bit of luck and lots of manœuvring that I could come and see you at all. Only Jean Huckmuir told me you had become a very magnificent person now, and quite different, and I somehow couldn't believe it. Are you different, Rose?"

"No. No; not really. Oh, *Susan*, don't believe that! Do people's outward surroundings ever change them to that extent? I saw Jean Huckmuir in Edinburgh; I'm sorry she thought me magnificent. I don't feel like that— and yet—it's all rather bewildering. I don't think anybody quite understands me."

"I do," said Susan. "I always do, and always shall, Rose. You're so honest that nothing insincere could ever get its claws into you. Now tell me, how far do your rolling acres extend? As far as the eye could see, as they always say in books?"

"Oh, dear me, no. You're bestowing about three-quarters of Fife on me, instead of a house and a park and a few fields."

"That seems to me enough for one person, darling."

"It is. But it doesn't bother me. There are factors and keepers always worrying away at my bit of earth."

" Absolutely yours? And you can do as you like with it?"

" Well—in a way. There are complications and modifications."

" Ah, I knew there would be something. You mean, you *can't* do as you like?"

" Far from it."

" Heavens, what a world! Are you happy?"

" Absolutely," said Lady Rose, after the slightest hesitation. " Are you?"

" No. I haven't got anything I want."

" Do you want very much to get married?"

" Well, yes; but I want a lot of other things as well. I wouldn't want that to be the end. And I wouldn't want to get married unless I fell in love, and that would be sure to be disastrous; it always is. Nobody in our world has ever yet fallen in love without its being completely unsuitable, from the days when King Cophetua chose a beggar-maid. Only in those times they accepted the situation, and now they don't. It isn't worth it. I should like more than anything in the world to belong to the middle classes. They fall in love, and marry who they like, and become nurses, and write books."

" All of them?" said Rose. " It does sound interesting."

Susan shrugged her shoulders. " Have you a girl among your children?"

" Yes. She's only four."

" Then I hope she grows up into a world where she won't either have to be an old maid, or marry somebody ' suitable '. I hope she'll be free; a free soul. I hope she'll be happier than either you or me, Rose."

" But I'm happy, Susan. What more could I need?"

Susan tied her bonnet-strings. " You haven't deceived me."

There was an awkward silence, while the chimes of a clock slowly struck four.

" Oh, Susan, you're not going? You must have tea."

" I can't. I have a hired carriage, and I must get the train to Edinburgh this evening. I haven't told you yet why I came. It was to say good-bye. I don't think you'll ever see me again."

" Why? Susan! Where are you going?"

Susan laughed. " Papa has been made a Colonial Governor. We sail next week for the West Indies. One of those ' pious ' islands."

" Pious!"

" Yes; with an unpronounceable saint's name. The sentence is for life. I shall learn to climb a palm-tree for my food, and run for my life at the first hint of a native rebellion."

" But it won't be a savage place, surely? "

" Savage enough. The last three Governors have died

in ten years, of catalepsy, cold steel, and sheer fright—in
that order. And everybody on the island is *crawling* with
a particularly rabid kind of yellow fever."

"*Everybody?*"

"Every man, woman, and child."

"Did the Queen say you must go?"

"Yes, my child. It is for the Empire. 'What though
the soldier knew someone had blundered; theirs not to
reason why——'"

"You'll come back again, Susan; you'll come and see
me again, and stay."

"That ocean, Rose; weeks in a rolling ship! Can you
imagine it?"

"So I've found you again, only to lose you?"

"Yes, but you're safe. You may be in a spacious,
magnificent prison, Rose, but you're safe. Nothing can
happen to you. There are layers and layers of protective
padding between you and all the things that happen in
the world; the dangerous things, the exciting things."

"You sound as though it were my fault!"

"No. Your misfortune, Rose. And mine too. Oh, if
ever I should come to earth again! Good-bye, and bless
you a thousand times!"

"You really wouldn't like to see the children?"

"I may as well be frank—no. Good-bye, my own
Rose."

149

"Good-bye, Susan, and may you be happy, and find what you want."

"On the savage island with the pious name?"

"Who knows! Good-bye!"

"Mamma, where's Daddy? He said I was to show him my copy-book," shouted Alastair.

"Daddy has gone to Redlace, darling. He had to see the keepers before his guests come on the twelfth."

"Oh! When's he coming back?"

"Not until Friday."

"Friday! Oh, Mamma! Cheers!"

"You shouldn't say that, Alastair," said Archie gravely. "Should he, Mamma?" At nine years of age Archie, with his dark, serious eyes, was rather sweet in his attention to correct behaviour.

"Who wants to come with me to feed the doves?" suggested Rose diplomatically.

"Me! Me! All of us!"

"Fee' de doves," announced Mary-Jean in her cooing baby voice. She was the loveliest four-year-old in the world, very like her mother, and with the sweetest disposition.

"I wonder just why God made doves," said Alastair. "He'd got pigeons already."

"But doves are just a bit of an improvement on pigeons," said Archie. "I like their fluffy feet."

" F'uffy feet," echoed Mary-Jean. " Pitty."

" Let me give them the corn, Mamma," begged Archie.

" No, Mamma; me!" clamoured Alastair.

Rose gave each child a handful of corn, and drew back to admire the exquisite picture; the glorious white background of Keepsfield, and the green and gold, blue and rose of the formal garden; the strutting birds like snowballs, and the three eager children: Archie, heir to Keepsfield and Redlace, the richest and most privileged little boy in Scotland, with his handsome head, tall straight body and graceful, deliberate gestures, sailor-suited like Alastair—though Alastair was short for seven and inclined to be plump—fair, and with the most fascinating dimples of which he would be horribly ashamed when he went to school; and Mary-Jean, that pink and golden baby with her white organdi frock and sash, and the silver bangles on her fat, delicious wrists. Cooing like the doves themselves, she attempted to seize and cuddle one unfortunate bird. Archie flew to the rescue; Mary-Jean looked rueful, and Rose suggested they should all go indoors for it was nearly bed-time.

" When I'm ten," said Archie, " may I stay up till ten o'clock?"

" And when he's eleven," chimed Alastair, " can he stay up till eleven o'clock; and when he's twelve can he stay up till twelve o'clock; and—oh, Mamma, what happens after you're twelve?"

Rose laughed. At the moment she felt deliciously free and happy. The sun was shining, the house she loved was all hers, and she had her adored children. She must make the most of these few days.

"I'd like a gun like Daddy's," said Archie.

"Not at nine, my child."

"I'm a bit tired of being nine," said Archie. "You don't get much."

"Oh, Archie! You had two puppies this year, and the big engine, and the skates——"

"And a ferret," put in Alastair, "but it died. It wasn't so healthy as most ferrets."

"I didn't know he had a ferret," said Rose. "He wasn't supposed to."

"I just called it mine," confessed Archie ruefully. "It was Rob's really. It was an awfully *sweet* ferret; p'raps that was because it wasn't feeling very well."

"Chockies," said Mary-Jean.

"She had four chockies last night," explained Alastair hastily, "and she was nearly sick, but not quite. Nanny was awfu' cross."

"It seems funny," said Archie, "to think you were a little girl here, Mamma. Were you here when you were nine, like me? Was it ages ago? Can you remember?"

"Oh, Archie!" cried Rose. "I can remember it perfectly well. I remember my sixth birthday, just as if it was yesterday. I had a Shetland pony and cart from my Mamma, and six gold sovereigns from Papa."

"Your Mamma is our Granny," said Archie. "She lives at Doune. She might give us a Shetland pony, only I'd rather have a huge horse. I could ride a horse here."

"We'll always live here, won't we, Mamma?" asked Alastair.

"Well, for a long time yet I hope, darling."

"I hope so. It's lovely here—by ourselves."

Rose frowned. Alastair was very much her child, rather frighteningly like her in mind and heart, and sometimes a little too outspoken.

"Let's race to the house," she said briskly. "Mary-Jean gets a half-way start—run along, darling pet, to the goldfish pond—Alastair can go as far as those white roses, and Archie starts from here. There are no prizes——"

"But the winner sits on the arm of Queen Mary's chair while you read, Mamma!" shouted Archie, who always coveted this position.

They raced, and Alastair won. Rose privately thought she had given him too much start. They all went into the great hall laughing. There was a new treasure there now; an alabaster head of Archie on a pedestal, done by a well-known sculptor. It was beautiful, and the children admired

it immensely and always stopped to say, " Hullo, Archie!
You haven't got any legs." This was a great joke.

" And now for our book!" shouted Archie, dashing up
the marble stairs to the Gallery. Alastair was after him
like a flash, to turn Queen Mary's chair to the light.

Rose sat down and took Mary-Jean on her knee; the
little golden head was already bobbing with sleepiness.
Alastair perched on the arm he had won; Archie crouched
on the floor and hugged his Mamma's ankles.

" What shall I read, darlings?"

" Water Babies!"

" Ooh, don't *shout*. Mary-Jean, what do you want to
hear?"

" Ickle Tom."

She read in a clear, lilting voice from the old copy that
Mr. Kingsley had given her nineteen years ago. The
children had heard the story so often that they knew pages
of it by heart. She could even see Alastair's lips moving
over the familiar words; but they never grew tired of it.
What a peach of a skin that child had!

It was growing too dark to see in the Gallery.

" Just the birds at Allfowlsness!" pleaded Archie.

" All right. But that must be the very, very last."

Nurse appeared. The children gave one despairing
glance, and then hurled themselves upon Rose, kissing her
to death.

SYLVIA SALISBURY

SHE READ IN A CLEAR, LILTING VOICE

" My angels! My precious pets! Oh . . . have mercy!
Alastair!

" Mamma! He isn't coming back till Friday, is he?
Say it's true!"

She jumped up. " Good night, children. Go with
Nanny, and if you're bad and throw the pillows about
instead of going to sleep I won't read to you for a whole
week!"

" Oh, yes, you will," said Archie shrewdly. " You
like it as much as we do."

" You're a rascal."

" So was Prince Charlie," put in Alastair. " Only *I'm*
more like the picture at Holyrood; Archie is dark, I'm fair."

" Wallace was dark!" insisted Archie. They raced off,
arguing happily, and Nanny followed, carrying the rosy,
sleep-flushed Mary-Jean.

Rose stood in the Gallery with her hands to her temples.
She mustn't . . . She mustn't feel like this, that it was a
reprieve when he went away; that a cloud lifted. And
Alastair—too discerning for seven years old—must be
checked. He was such a good man too, was Hector; such
a marvellous landlord, such a perfect host, so above reproach in his public and private life. Ten years she had
been married to him; ten years her warm, impulsiveness
had been chained to his frigidity. Sir Hector Galowrie
was consistently correct; he never had an emotion, not

because his nature was phlegmatic, but because emotion
was vulgar and must be repressed until repression became
second nature. The loving, glowing Rose had beaten her
soft hands against cold granite; then she gave up beating
and drew away, and hid her warmth until she was alone
with the children. Ten years . . . such a long, long time,
when you were used to being loved, and wanted to be
loved, and were made to feel that your cordiality was un-
dignified and your joy in living mere bad behaviour. Sir
Hector Galowrie had never forgiven Queen Victoria for
making Rose Countess of Lochlule in her own right, or
Rose for presuming to wear that title and its implications.
To be Lady Galowrie should be enough for his wife. He
had the strongest opinions about the respective status of
husband and wife. He had married Lady Rose Targenet
to get Keepsfield; and the fact that the servants at Keepsfield persisted in regarding Rose as their mistress and himself as her consort galled him cruelly. Of course, to all
outward appearances they were a perfect couple, very
much admired in Scottish society, and great favourites of
the Queen when she came to Balmoral.

Rose could never forget how on one occasion a few
months after they were married she had exchanged a little
joke at table with Colinby, the butler, and they had both
laughed. Sir Hector immediately ordered Colinby from
the room, and when the door was closed said, "Rose!

Have you completely forgotten yourself, to joke with a servant?" "But, Hector!" Her eyes were wide, and still full of laughter. "I've joked with Colinby since I was ten. I think the world of him."

"*Of the butler!* Will you *please* have a little respect for my name, and remember your own dignity in future."

She bit her lip. "I'm sorry, but we've always treated our upper servants like friends. They don't presume. I can't be a human iceberg."

He knit his fingers in a way she learned to hate.

"You are Lady Galowrie now. One more exhibition and I shall dismiss Colinby."

"You can't. He's my servant."

"I can and I shall. We could even live at Redlace."

She had cried on her bed all the afternoon, realizing bitterly that in 1874 married women had no rights, even if they were countesses. She didn't cry now, for she had the children, and in any case crying did no good after ten years. In his way Hector was good to her, too. He admired his handsome children and approved of her for having produced them in the decorous and imperceptible fashion of mid-Victorian society. He had given her an elegant diamond brooch when Archie, the heir, was born; ear-rings to match for Alastair; and a hair ornament for Mary-Jean. He had never kissed her, except in the formal salute demanded by courtesy, cold lips against a cool cheek.

Sometimes there was a fierce fire in her heart that frightened her and made her tremble, for she did not know what it could be. She was twenty-nine now, but she looked a young girl. She tried to make herself look older by dressing her hair and wearing black lace scarves. Romping with the children she was just nineteen; nineteen and unawakened, a passionate, crimson-hearted Rose on which the sun had never laid his life-giving caress. Even the conceiving and bearing of her children had been achieved with the formality demanded by Sir Hector Galowrie in his domestic affairs. . . .

He was coming back on Friday; Wednesday, Thursday, Friday. It was Friday. Sir Hector had arrived at Keepsfield and gone to his study. He sent for the children to greet him and asked about their lessons. Rose carried in Mary-Jean. Archie had no fear of his father; he was the heir, and knew himself to be privileged.

"Daddy! When can I go and shoot with you at Redlace?"

"When you are sixteen, Archie."

"Oh, what a long time."

"You must go to school first. What does Mr. Massingham say about your lessons?"

"He said my Latin was very good."

"I'm gratified. Did you have your riding lesson? Are you keeping your hands down better?"

" Yes, Daddy. When can I have my own horse?"

" You shall have one for Christmas."

Alastair shrieked. " Oh! Me too! Oh, Daddy! Mamma! A horse!"

" *Alastair!* " thundered Sir Hector. The child was abruptly silent.

" Rose, this child is hysterical. He should be confined to his room until he can control himself."

" Oh, Hector, really! He's only seven, and he was excited about Archie's horse."

" Then he has no business to be excited. He isn't a ploughman's son. Did you rewrite that disgraceful copy, Alastair? The spelling was atrocious."

" No, Daddy, I forgot."

Sir Hector rose, shrugging his shoulders.

" That settles it. The child is growing up uncontrolled and slovenly. I shall send him away to school, next term."

Rose protested. " No! Why, he's only little. He's far too young. You can't."

" He shall go, and Archie too. They're both getting spoilt and womanized. There's a preparatory school at Perth; I shall make inquiries to-morrow. And can't that child walk, Rose, that you have to carry her? I object to seeing you doing a nursemaid's work. Come to me, Mary-Jean."

Mary-Jean, secure in her beauty, went to her father

without fear and seized his gold hunter watch with a delighted chuckle. He patted her yellow head.

"There, there. She certainly is an attractive child. I want you to go with me to the Gilmour's this afternoon, Rose. The carriage will be ready at three."

Rose read to the children that night with a heavy heart. Archie stroked the carving of the ancient chair, fingered the worn velvet, and asked to be told the old stories of Queen Mary. Then he said proudly, "I'm going away to school, Daddy said so."

"Do you want to go so soon, Archie?"

"I think so. Then I shall soon be grown up and I can go to Daddy's shoots. And I'm to have a *horse* at Christmas."

Alastair suddenly burst into tears. Rose was crying a little herself as she hugged his flaxen head. His fingers dug her wrist painfully.

"Mamma, don't let me go to school! Please, Mamma! I want to stay with you! I'm frightened. Oh, Mamma, I'll be frightened at school."

"He's a baby," said Archie.

"Oh, Archie, don't say that, darling! It's unkind to Alastair."

"Poor Al'stair," said Mary-Jean suddenly.

"Come, children, say good-night," whispered Rose as Nurse appeared at the door of the Gallery. Archie went bounding off; he was in high spirits. Alastair hung back, and then followed the others slowly with fair head hung down.

The Countess of Lochlule sat alone in the great carved chair in the twilight of the Gallery. Beyond her long windows was a primrose sky, and one luminous star that quivered above the sea. Like an unhappy Queen who had once sat in this same chair, she looked out to the horizon of Scotland. Her land; her home; these were her loves. This house, these stones, this polished wood with the waxen glimmer, this marble and velvet, this twilight hush, this air of ancient peace—in all that was Keepsfield was her heart rooted. Her long chiffon sleeves fell to the floor; her head was lifted and her face softly alight. She was afraid—afraid that something was to be taken from her. In all the years, each evening she had gathered the children to her knee at this chair, had told them the old stories, taught them their earliest lessons of chivalry and truth, given them heroes to worship, lighted her own enthusiasms in their bright eyes. And was it all over? So soon! Were children so young to be taken out into the world of men, to learn other lessons, to be hardened, to divide their hearts and worship other loves? Ah, but they loved Scotland and Keepsfield, and no one could ever break that early spell. And perhaps when they grew up they would come again to gather at Queen Mary's chair.

Sir Hector left on Monday. It was the 10th of August, and a large party of men were to assemble next day for the shooting at Redlace. He was anxious that everything should be in order and intended to make a personal tour of inspection over his estate.

It was a glorious day. Rose had taken the children for a walk by the sea, and they had been fascinated by the sapphire waters and emerald reflections of the Firth of Forth as they chased along the sand-dunes. They had tea in the yew garden and proceeded to tell stories. This story-game was always popular. Rose would begin, and after working up to a point of great excitement would hand the narrative over to Archie, who carried on to his heart's content and always managed to introduce a battle or duel. Meanwhile, Alastair would be bobbing up and down with eagerness for his turn. He was highly imaginative, and often very funny, and would watch his audience anxiously for signs of appreciation, which he rewarded by wilder flights of fiction. Mary-Jean was still at the " listener only " stage; so the story would pass back to Rose, and then in its turn to the two boys, over and over, until they were all tired with laughing and clapping and excitement.

" And so," concluded Rose, triumphantly, " the shepherd came back to his native hills and settled down to mind his sheep, and lived happily ever after."

"Until his next adventure," suggested Archie.

"Well, we're certainly not going to have that to-day! It's six o'clock."

"To-night at the chair," said Archie, "we'll have some battles where we beat the English."

"We *always* beat the English," said Alastair hotly.

"Not at Bannockburn."

"That was murder; Duncan says so. Wasn't it, Mamma?"

"You children are the fiercest little Scots I ever saw!"

"Nannie's brother," said Alastair, "can make a noise like water going down the bath."

"Plunk!" said Mary-Jean. "Plunky. Plunky."

"Oh, Mamma! She's trying to do it. Isn't she funny?"

Rose thought: "How empty, how desolate when they go away." They fitted into her magic, summer world. They were—though she did not know it—an insurance against some hunger of the heart that lay too deep for curious introspection.

Colinby was coming to them across the lawns. He said, "May I speak to you, my lady?"—with a glance at the children.

"Certainly, Colinby. Now, children, I want you to run to the greenhouses and choose me the loveliest carnation that Cameron has there. Tell him I sent you; and be sure it is the loveliest."

Colinby looked after the three little running figures till they dived into a yew alley and were gone.

"My lady, there is some bad news. I am deeply regretful to have to prepare you. It is from Redlace."

She turned in her chair, looked into his fine eyes, and away again.

"Sir Hector?"

"Yes, my lady. There has been an accident."

"He is——? Oh, Colinby, you needn't tell me."

"Yes, my lady. He is dead."

"Come to the house."

She rose, and led the way steadily to the house, up the long marble steps to a small room that opened from the terrace. The butler followed.

"Now, Colinby, please tell me exactly what happened." She was seated, very dignified, pale and still.

"My lady, shortly after his arrival he was walking through a plantation with one of the keepers. Some poacher had set a snare, and the keeper caught his foot in it in the long grass. He fell, and his gun went off. The charge entered the chest of Sir Hector, who was close behind. He died before they could bring a doctor."

There was a long silence.

"Thank you, Colinby. You've been most considerate."

It was like the Countess, he said to himself, to be so thoughtful, even in a personal moment like this, as though she guessed how he had dreaded his task and might later reproach himself for his inadequacy.

" Shall I send someone to you, my lady?"

" No, thank you; I see the children are coming. Leave them with me."

The three children came springing across the lawns, kindly hanging back to help Mary-Jean negotiate the difficult steps with her fat little legs. Then they all bounded in.

" Why did you come indoors, Mamma? We thought you were hiding."

" Look, Mamma, isn't it the most beautiful pinky-pink carnation?"

" It was quite the loveliest of all," said Alastair, nearly stammering with excitement; " because Cameron said it was called *Lady Rose*, after you!"

What if Heaven be, that, fair and strong
At life's best, with our eyes upturned
Whither life's flower is first discerned,
    We, fixed so, ever should so abide?
What if we still ride on, we two,
With life for ever old, yet new,
Changed not in kind but in degree,
The instant made eternity,—
And Heaven just prove that I and she
    Ride, ride together, forever ride?

ROBERT BROWNING.

CHAPTER VII

"OH!" said Helen Dacre; and stopped abruptly. The old caretaker was looking away across the green, waving park, her eyes a little wrinkled against the sun, her hands lying loosely on the worn black lap of her dress.

"How can I express myself?" Helen stumbled on. "I mean—when her husband was dead. I picture her living on here with the children and nothing ever breaking her peace. It should have been like that—but from your face I see—I feel—it was different. You're going to tell me that something dreadful happened!"

"Yes," said the old woman reluctantly, "something dreadful happened." She slowly drew the back of one hand across her temples, smoothing the blown strands of silvered hair; and went on. "It was dreadful—because of those days she lived in. Even to-day, with all their free, modern ways, it would have been considered most unconventional; but then it was a sin past forgiveness. You must remember that she was a Scottish peeress, and Sir

Hector was the head of a leading family, and they were both popular in society and favoured by the Queen. And in those days aristocracy was aristocracy and standards were high; to offend was to be cast out. It was the height of the Victorian period; the rules of correct behaviour were rigid."

" But what did she *do*?" said Helen. " I simply can't foresee what you are going to say."

" She was married again," said Mrs. Memmary simply, " within three months of her husband's death—and to a most unsuitable person."

" Wait!" said Helen. " Who ever he was—she loved him. It was love this time, the one love of her life. I know it."

" How did you know?"

" Because everything has led up to this. A woman so alive and so loving as Lady Rose couldn't go all her life without a lover. Who was he, please?"

" He was a nobody," said Mrs. Memmary. " A young man she met in a public park; an accountant's clerk from an office in Edinburgh."

Helen's face glowed; she pressed her hands to her cheeks with an impulsive gesture.

" I'm glad!" she cried. " It was noble of her."

Mrs. Memmary lowered her gaze; her lips seemed to tighten.

"You think that? *You* can look at it like *that*? How very different the times are now."

"But," cried Helen, "any sane person would look at it like that! What did it matter about his social position so long as she loved him, and he was good—worthy of Lady Rose, who was so sweet herself?"

"That is the modern outlook."

"Indeed it is! All these bogies of social position are being swept away; and people are realizing that man made a chain for himself when he made convention. Convention! *They say!* Provided there is no moral principle involved, I say convention should never stand in the way of an individual's happiness."

The old woman shook her head.

"Then you will never be able to understand the feeling of those times, the accumulated horror of social remonstrance that made Lady Rose an outcast, an exile for life."

Helen Dacre gave an exclamation.

"You don't mean it was *that* that sent her to the Continent—for life!"

"It was that. She gave up the world for love; and society saw that she lost everything. Her home——"

"They couldn't take this place from her!"

"But they could make it impossible for her to live here. To meet frozen faces wherever she went; to know that she was the most notorious woman in Scotland; to be banished from Court——"

" Oh! Oh, how terrible! And the children?"

" Their father's mother took them away. The heir had to be brought up on his own estates in any case; and the relatives got a legal ruling that their mother was an improper person to have charge of the younger children."

" Because she married the man she loved!"

" Because she broke the law of society," said Mrs. Memmary.

" And were you here at the time all this happened?"

" Yes. I was here then."

" But what did *you* think about it?"

" There was something to be said for both sides. There always is, even in bitter argument."

" Is that all you thought of it? What was the view of the other servants?"

" They were not asked to express an opinion, madam."

" Oh! What dreadful days! What cruel, hide-bound, callous, intolerant, bigoted, hypocritical, tyrannical days! Poor Lady Rose, did it break her heart?"

" On the contrary," said Mrs. Memmary. " She was so happy that no earthly consideration could have touched her. She was above the earth; she was in love."

" He must have been wonderful," said Helen with shining eyes. " Did you ever see him?"

"Yes, madam. I did."

"What was he like? Please!"

There was a long pause; the old woman was considering. She looked at the brilliant lawns, at the blue sky, at the golden shivers of light that ran in the leaves of the trees.

"Why, he was like a summer's day," she said, as though she had just discovered the idea, and the words to clothe it.

"Oh, that's perfect. And what was his name?"

"I never heard Lady Rose call him anything but Morie. I think his name was Moray, but why his mother should want to give a child a name like that is past my guessing."

"Perhaps," said Helen wickedly, "she was *not* an admirer of Queen Mary."

"Perhaps," said Mrs. Memmary drily, "she was not a true Scot!"

"But you said they were happy," said Helen. "That is much better. Did they run away?"

"You might call it that. They went to Italy, and Keepsfield was closed."

"And then?"

"And then the years went by and the evil days came; and you see for yourself how things are now."

"You mean—that was the end of Lady Rose's story? It seems a vague, disappointing ending."

"Vague?" The old woman thought for a moment, and said, "But in real life things go like that. Our stories have no ending. We come into the light for a little while, and then we move away into the shadows and nobody sees us any more. It is better that way. We can live more quietly, and prepare for the Great Light beyond."

Helen nodded. " Do you know—I shall often think of her. Whenever I go to Italy I shall think of her, and when I see a lovely old woman with a Scottish face, and blue eyes, and a lace scarf, I shall wonder if she can be Lady Rose. Would her husband be there too?"

" Oh no," said Mrs. Memmary. " He is dead now."

" But he lived long enough to make her life worth while?"

" They had a long life together, so people say."

Helen leant forward with lightly clasped hands.

" I wish you could tell me how they met, and all about that first meeting. What a romance! Where and when it took place, and how she looked. It must have been love at first sight, a perfect romance."

The old woman sighed, and shook her head.

" Ah, now you've asked me more than I can tell."

" Of course. That is something I shall never know. Perhaps I can make up a story for myself, and picture it. You see, Mrs. Memmary, you've made Lady Rose live for me; you've told me all the little things and big things and *fairly* important things about her; and then when the great, stupendous, glorious Thing comes you can't tell me

174

anything more at all. But life is always like that, and imagination has such a capacity for making the unknowable beautiful. I ought to thank you for not telling me all; I do thank you."

"You seemed to understand," said Mrs. Memmary simply. "I liked to tell you."

Helen stood up, smiling.

"That is a compliment." She took one sweeping comprehensive glance at all the beauty around her. The afternoon was growing late, and the shadows of the elms lay in sable bands across the golden lawns. The sky was faintly flushed with coral, and a trail of homing birds went winging into the west.

"If she had only lived to-day," breathed Helen, "how happy she might have been. The past has many tragedies to answer for; lives that never need have been torn in two, as I think hers was torn. Are we kinder now? I think so, don't you, Mrs. Memmary? Once they wasted beauty or flung it away. They only recognized it in its prescribed forms; now we look for it in every circumstance, and are glad when we discover some unsuspected revelation."

The old woman flushed; then, as she turned her eyes from the sky to Helen's face, she said with a kind of burning confidence, "Beauty is never wasted, madam, and never flung away, for you can't destroy it. It always springs again for it's eternal; and I think you will own that to-day it is flowering here from the seeds Lady Rose sowed in her sorrow so many years ago."

Helen gazed. " And you call yourself just a caretaker!" she said.

In the portfolio of Time were leaves that Helen Dacre could never see. She wished that she could; she had expressed that wish, and then added that she must rely on her imagination. What kind of a scene that imagining painted for her one cannot tell. She may have come near the truth. More likely it is that she could not visualize anything quite so natural and simple as the meeting and falling in love of Rose and Morie. To look back upon it is to prove that innocence of evil intention may bring consequences just as dreadful as premeditated guilt. So the air is heavy with harsh words, and the thunder of denunciation has been heard across all the years since that September day.

1884

SEPTEMBER

It was a warm, golden September day when the Countess of Lochlule travelled to Edinburgh to visit her lawyers, Messrs. Crawford, Crawford and Nicholson. She was accompanied by her maid and her late husband's secretary; and a friend, Lady Emmery, had placed a house in the capital at her disposal for the few days that the visit might entail.

Rose had been a prisoner for a month since Sir Hector's death and elaborate funeral. Convention had garbed her in heavy black, had swathed her in crape and veils, and condemned her to closed and darkened rooms. That she should appear in public so soon as this was perhaps a little indiscreet, except that Rose was rather a privileged person and could be expected to do the right thing. Besides, she had the care of two large estates which required urgent attention; and in any case everybody who "mattered" was away in the Highlands. Rose's private reason for her journey to Edinburgh was that she couldn't bear this barbarity of widowhood a minute longer; she was like a lark in a narrow cage, her whole being crying out in revolt, crying for freedom, straining to soar into the sunlight. She could not grieve in her heart for Sir Hector, though she had sincerely tried to do so. Outwardly she had done her duty with a show of solemnity and mourning. Now—now!—the sun was warm on her face as she sat in the carriage, and even through the ugly, dragging veil she could see the mauve-blue sky soft and blooming over the Castle Rock, and the jagged etching of the old city roofs, and the battlements of Holyroodhouse. It was summer still, and she was alive, she was young! Such a song arose in her heart that she feared it would burst from her lips. What on earth would her whey-faced maid and the dour secretary think if they could read her mind? (Her first maid, Jean, had married years ago and left her for a cottage home at Dunbar.)

So they reached Emmery House. In the afternoon . . . "Your ladyship will want to rest," said her maid primly.

Rose, placed in a winged chair, her feet set on a stool, watched helpless while the curtains were drawn, shutting out the sweet, warm day. The room was stuffy and smelt of blankets and old wood.

"Is there anything else, m'lady?"

"No, thank you, Ann."

"Very good, m'lady. I shall be in the maids' parlour. The bell-cord is at your elbow, m'lady. I shall not disturb you till you ring."

"Thank you, Ann."

"I can't bear it! I won't bear it!" cried Rose's heart as the bars of the cage were closing.

She was on her feet; she had found a small, less heavy bonnet. No, she would not wear that terrible veil! She must go out, just to see the sun, the lovely, warming autumn sun.

She crossed Princes Street and went into the Gardens and sat down on a seat to watch the people. It was so interesting; it was life. The nurses, the children, the mothers, the soldiers, the lovers, all in the warm afternoon in that sheltered place under the Rock, with Arthur's Seat blue in the distance and a sky that seemed to reflect the purple of the heathery hills beyond the city.

She wondered about the people, studying their dress and overhearing scraps of conversation.

Was the tall sergeant, talking to the nursemaid, Seaforth or Gordon Highlanders? If the girl would only move a few inches she would be able to see his tartan . . .

" Gordon!" said a voice; a voice with a smile in it.

Rose started. It was the young man who had been sitting at the other end of her bench.

" I read your thoughts. Please forgive me. I was right, wasn't I?"

" You were. It was very clever of you."

" Not clever. Everybody looks that way when they're wondering about a tartan. But *you* should know them all."

" I? Why should I?"

" Because I know who you are. I've seen you riding in your carriage. You're Lady Galowrie, aren't you?"

Rose nodded. " I'm not pleased. I didn't want anybody to know me. It's so lovely not to be known."

" Then forget that I recognized you. *I don't even know you.* What *is* your name?"

" Rose. What is yours?"

" Andrew Moray Montmary. They call me Morie for short."

"Moray! What a dreadful name! Why did they call you that?"

"My mother's name was Moray, but she couldn't help it. She adored Queen Mary."

"That's better," said Rose. "I could even forgive you for being called Moray."

It was at this point that she looked at him closely for the first time; and it was probably even in that first moment she realized he was all her dreams come true; that golden young man with the clear brow and level grey eyes, the smooth tanned cheeks and firm yet tender lips above a well-cut chin. He was her portrait of Prince Charlie; the lover whose picture had lived in her heart. As for Andrew Moray Montmary, he had fallen in love with Lady Galowrie at first sight, three years ago. By now his passion for her had become second nature, but he had never dreamed that he would ever meet her. It was so impossible; she a great lady in society, he an accountant's clerk in an Edinburgh office. Of course he was just the kind of lad to fall madly in love with a beautiful woman whose carriage had stopped opposite him in a street crush; he was romantic, sensitive, high-souled, clever, a great reader. And he had been faithful to that image for three years, feeding his romance on occasional social paragraphs in the daily paper, till this divine, this heaven-sent afternoon had led him to a bench in Princes Street Gardens . . . it was unbelievable, yet here he was and there she was, exquisite flesh and spirit.

" Morie? " she said as soon as she found her breath.

" Rose!"

" You're like a picture in Holyroodhouse. Do you know the one I mean?"

" *Not* the Prince Charlie! Oh, Rose! My mother used to say so, and I thought it was just the usual, disgusting maternal flattery."

" You are like him."

" Rose, why are you in mourning?"

" Didn't you see it in the newspapers, a month ago?"

" No. I was in Skye a month ago, for my holiday."

" My husband is dead."

" Sir Hector Galowrie is dead!"

" Yes. I've come to Edinburgh to see my lawyers. I have a big estate to look after; two estates, one my own and one my husband's, for my little boy."

" How many children have you, Rose?"

" Three."

" You look so young, about twenty-two."

" I'm twenty-nine; I don't feel as though I had lived very much of my life."

" I'm thirty-one."

" Are you married?"

" No!" he thundered.

" You needn't be violent! "

" I am violent. I've only loved one woman in my life. I've been faithful to her image for three years, and you ask me am I married! "

" I'm sorry. Where is your home? "

" Here in Edinburgh. Just my mother and my sister and myself. I'm an accountant's clerk. "

" I don't *think* I know what that is. "

" You needn't know. "

" Tell me about Skye. I never went to the lovely wild places. "

" Oh, Rose, the lovely wild places! It'll take me hours to tell you; but we've got all our lives. "

" I feel, " said Rose slowly, " as though we'd known each other always. "

" That's what I meant, " said Morie gravely. " It is like two streams coming together—then—one river. "

" Tell me when you saw me first? "

" Sitting in your carriage in Princes Street in a traffic crush. I was so close I could have touched you. It was three years ago. "

" I'm glad you didn't touch me. I'd rather have waited for us to meet, like this. "

" I think it was Fate. "

" I know it was! "

" *Rose!* "

They were in that state in which every word is full of meaning, every glance sets the heart hammering; a touch would be so ecstatic that one dare not contemplate it yet, but it is coming! And the magic moments draw nearer to fulfilment.

"I must go," said Rose, terrified of her heart.

"Won't you walk with me as far as the Castle and back again? It's such a lovely afternoon," he pleaded.

"I should *like* to," she said doubtfully.

"Then come."

"Shouldn't you be in some—office?"

He grimaced, and said rather shamefacedly, "They gave me an afternoon off to go and visit a dentist."

"And did you?"

"Yes. He hurt abominably. Listen, it's only four o'clock. What time must you be in?"

What time must she be in! That decided Rose; she would walk to the Castle. Why should she go home for *anybody*, if she didn't want to? She was the Countess of Lochlule and accountable to no one—except perhaps to the Queen, and that was a vague sort of accountability.

There was a little breeze on the Rock; it was delicious. They leaned on the parapet and felt in their new, secret joy that they owned the enchanted city spread below, and all enchanted lands. They didn't say a word—yet. She didn't even ask him who was the lady he had loved and been faithful to for three years. In her heart she knew.

They said good-bye, and Rose went back to her borrowed house in a cab. The next day she would see her lawyers, and meet Morie again in the Gardens at five o'clock.

They met, and he took her to Arthur's Seat and told her that he loved her.

" I love you too," said Rose. " I've loved you all my life."

" My beautiful girl! My Rose!"

" Oh, Morie, my darling."

" People wouldn't believe that things could happen like this in real life."

" I could believe anything. I've always believed that *the* most beautiful thing will happen if you want it hard enough."

" But what can we do now? You're you, and I'm me, and our ordinary lives are so far apart."

" We can get married, Morie."

" You mean that? You'd marry *me*?"

" Yes. I don't think I can ever make you understand; but this was meant for me. All my life this day has been coming nearer, and I never knew. I was blind, or perhaps just asleep. Other people knew, Morie. I remember two people; one came just before I married Hector. She told me I should wake, and live. I didn't understand, but she was so wise. She's dead now. And I have a friend, Susan Jardine; she has gone across the sea, and I don't suppose I shall ever see her again; but only a few weeks ago—it seems like a lifetime!—we talked about life and happiness, and the imprisonment of the soul. She wanted to escape; she wanted me to escape, only she didn't think there would ever be a way. She said love was always unsuitable. But when it comes, Morie, it is the door into Life, and you must go through. Why shouldn't we be married?"

"Rose, if you'll marry me I'll take care of you for ever, in my own way. It won't be the way you're accustomed to. Will it be good enough? I've loved you like loving a dream for three years; now I love you in life. Suppose you don't like what I give you? If you should think it cheap and common——"

"I want it common, Morie. I want love, common and gloriously common. All the things you give me will be so lovely that I shall want to cry when I see you offering them with your outstretched hands. This all began when I was a child and loved a picture."

"Oh, Rose! God knows, I'm not a picture! I'm not a Prince of the Realm. I may have a face like his, but I'm of the people, strong and hot-headed, passionately in love and abominably poor. You're breakable. I hardly dare take you in my hands."

"Take me in your arms, Morie! Break me if you like, but not any of your promises."

"Oh, my dear! What shall I do? I haven't any money. I've two old miniatures that my father left me; that's all of value."

"I've plenty of money. It doesn't mean anything to me, Morie."

"It's worse than that. You're a Countess."

"As if that were anything!"

"I say, you're a Countess!"

"I'm not. I'm your girl, Rose. Do you *want* to marry me?"

"I want to marry you to-day. Now. Here. If you leave me now I'll lose you. I'll be afraid. We can't wait, Rose; we dare not."

They were married three weeks later in Edinburgh by a registrar. There were probably in the whole of Scotland no two people more deeply and single-heartedly in love. After those first hesitating moments of feeling their ground, their relative social positions and the question of money never entered their heads. Rose made a large settlement on her husband on their wedding-day, and that was the end of that. They sincerely believed that they had been meant for each other since the day they were born; so in all probability they had.

They went north for their honeymoon, to a little lodge

in the forest near Bonar, and Rose took three reliable servants from Keepsfield. Now they had so much to tell each other; and a long time and such beautiful places to tell it in, sitting out bareheaded in the autumn-clad forest, with the breath of the pines on their lips, and the mountain air flowing down like wine. There are honeymoons and honeymoons; some rapturous and some overrated, but can there be one to compare with the honeymoon of a woman who has known ten years of marriage without love, and now finds her perfect lover beside her in a Highland forest in the purple-and-golden fall of the year? In those two weeks Rose reached to the full height of rapture of which humanity is capable. Morie was as beautiful and as dear as her imagined dreams of him.

Rose went away a radiant and beloved woman; she came back to find herself a branded outcast, without honour in her own country, her own home, among her own people. The scandal had raged during her absence. Rose's mother had descended from her house at Doune, taken Mary-Jean back with her, and given orders that her daughter was not to be admitted. That, however, did not prevent her from writing several well-worded letters, the meaning of which was unmistakable; for the Dowager Countess belonged to a generation which had not only brought letter-writing to a fine art, but possessed a command of opprobrious phraseology undreamed of in these moderate days. The first was handed to Rose before she had removed her bonnet.

LICHTS ABBEY,
DOUNE,
October 26th, 1884

MY DEAR ROSE,

I have given instructions that this letter be presented to you on your arrival at the house you have defamed, but which owing to circumstances over which I have no control is still your property. I advise you to remain in it, and not to attempt to show your face to the society you have *outraged.* This is probably the most disastrous letter that any mother has ever had to write to any daughter. I am shattered and brought low. I shall never raise my head again. Can it be Fate alone, or through some fault of mine that my one child, raised and nurtured for high position and noble honours should have made *Shipwreck* of every *Principle* in a manner that would be indecent in a maid-servant? Of the future I will not write; alas! I can see for you nothing but remorse and shame. Were you mad, Rose? God help you when you come to your senses!

Mary-Jean is with me. I have told her she no longer has a mother. The boys are with their paternal grandmother at Redlace. Lady Galowrie refuses to hold any communication with you. May God forgive you for Scotland cannot.

Your sorrowing and afflicted mother,
MARGARET JANE LOCHLULE

" Poor Mamma! " was all Rose said. She had counted the cost and had expected just this. Only the last phrase rankled like a thorn in her mind. " God forgive you for Scotland cannot."

"What have I done to Scotland?" cried Rose in bitter indignation. "Hector was dead and I never loved him; but I did my duty while he was alive. And Scotland should be proud to give me a man like Morie for my husband. Nobody understands; nobody tries to understand."

Then she heard that steps were being taken to remove the children from her care, as an improper person to have charge of young people of such high rank and future position.

"I shall appeal to the Queen!" protested Rose to Mr. Crawford at Edinburgh.

The lawyer turned pale. "Your ladyship would be ill-advised to attempt any such thing."

Rose was sensitive enough not to pursue the matter. It would have been an unpleasant task for the lawyer to have to tell her to her face the Queen had given strict orders that the name of the Countess of Lochlule should never again be breathed within the walls of Balmoral or Windsor. Rose's crime had been almost a personal affront to the Royal widowhood.

Rose wrote to the children, but she had little hope that her letters would be delivered. Children forgot so quickly, and were so easily influenced and prejudiced.

Then one day a footman spoke insolently to Morie. Morie went white. It was the culmination of a hundred little disloyalties on the part of the newer servants. Rose had noticed it. She sent for Colinby and gave orders for the footman to be dismissed, but she knew that this was more an admission of weakness than a solution.

" We shall have to go away," said Rose. " Just for a little while, until this has blown over."

They were sitting clasped together, cheek against cheek, on the edge of the great carved bed in Rose's room.

" Oh, God!" said Morie wretchedly. " I've done all this to you."

" Not a bit," said Rose briskly. " I counted the cost, and I loved you enough. I love you enough to let everything go but you; just my actual life and yours, those are the only precious things."

" I'm getting afraid for you, darling."

" Why? You needn't be."

" You're doing all the suffering and the giving, that's why."

" But that's my affair, Morie. I knew all this would happen. I told you so, even when we were at Bonar, but we agreed not to talk about it then."

" Not *all* this, Rose. It has been worse than you ever thought."

" They can't take you from me. In the old days they used to burn men for their faith. They couldn't take the faith from them, so it wasn't much satisfaction, and the martyrs didn't care."

Morie sprang up. " But, God in Heaven, Rose, what do you think of me? I'm a man. I should be giving and suffering; and instead of that I'm taking, and leaving the strife to you. If I can't get into the fight I shall smash this place with my fists. I live here, day after day, furious against those who persecute you; and I can't do anything. It's enough to drive a man mad. I am a man, Rose; and yet here I sit, flesh and bone and blood, passion and love and hatred, no more able to work for you and comfort you than if I were in prison. This *is* prison—a cold gaol for both of us, Rose."

" Keepsfield? Prison! Oh, Morie, it is; you're right. We can't even love each other properly here. Why— why?" In her heart she was already making plans, tremendous decisions.

" If we could have stayed for ever in the forest at Bonar, Rose, where values were natural and uncomplicated. I love you so terribly that I'm trying all the time to reconcile two worlds in my heart, that one and this. It's a tearing struggle."

" It shan't go on. We'll go to Italy. We'll have beauty and sunshine, and we won't hurry back. The winter will go by, and Time alters everything. We'll take Colinby with us; he would never leave me."

So they went to Italy; but they never came back. The passing of Time made things not easier but more difficult.

Colinby went with them, and stayed with them for years, in fact until he died. At the end Rose could only pay him a small salary, for the war had decimated her income, and old standards and values were crashing.

Colinby did not care about the money; he was the most loyal of all her servants and died an exile, in her service at the little villa at Ragusa where for nearly half a century Rose and Morie were lovers.

Wherever beauty has been quick in clay
Some effluence of it lives, a spirit dwells
  .   .   .   .   .   .

Then at a turn, a word, an act, a thought,
Such difference comes; the spirit apprehends
That place's glory; for where beauty fought
Under the veil the glory never ends;
But the still grass, the leaves, the trembling flower
Keep, through dead time, that everlasting hour.

JOHN MASEFIELD

CHAPTER VIII

THE afternoon was late, and a tiny breeze shimmered over the grass. A sighing like music ran among the leaves, and through the trees the distant sky was all golden and very deep.

" And so she went away for ever," said Helen Dacre. "That is all. No end to the story; all imagined. We can't follow her. I think it was worth while. You see, for her the story didn't end; perhaps it was just beginning."

" Like in the story-books," said Mrs. Memmary. " And so they lived happily ever after!"

Helen shook her head. " Not quite like that. She would have so many memories. Perhaps—regrets? How I do wonder! I shall always wonder. I wish she could have come back here in the end; it would have been more fitting."

" Come back here to die, you mean?"

" No. To live for ever—almost. To complete the circle."

" But Keepsfield! That sale-board at the gates——"

LADY ROSE AND MRS. MEMMARY

"I know." Helen Dacre rose to her feet, and said reluctantly, "I must go. The men are tired of waiting. I
shall never forget to-day. I little thought when we came
this way so casually——"

"You may come again, madam."

"No. I don't suppose I shall ever come again; it would
spoil everything. Perhaps you won't understand, Mrs.
Memmary, but to-day hasn't been quite real; all the magnificence and the peace, and the beauty, and sitting here
with you talking about Lady Rose. To-morrow it will be a
dream, and later—well, something I read in a book or saw
in a play, something lovely and quite unforgettable, locked
up in the inner, inexpressible part of me. I shall be back
in London too—another world, a long way away."

"Not just the miles, madam."

"No. How perceptive you are! I don't know how to
thank you."

"To thank *me*?"

"For everything; for what you told me, your confi-
dences. The story was wrapped around your life. Lady
Rose was *your* friend."

The two men were approaching. "You've been here
quite long enough, Helen you gossip!" her husband called,
laughing. "It's getting late and we suggested an early
dinner if you remember."

"She doesn't remember anything," said Van Elsen,

196

reading the look in Helen's eyes. "She's enchanted. 'Weave a circle round her thrice . . .'"

Dacre smiled pleasantly at the old woman, who stood with folded hands against the white balustrade, her eyes a little wrinkled against the level sun, her thin silver hair lifted by a warm and languorous breeze.

"You've been very kind." He slipped something into the fold of her fingers. "I wish we could have taken the house. Perhaps somebody will soon. Shall you——" he was going to say "be pleased", but some inexplicable impulse made him change it to "shall you mind?"

She had already become the impersonal servant again.

"It would be a very good thing, sir."

"What would happen to you?"

"To me, sir?"

"They wouldn't want a caretaker, would they?"

"They might let me stay on, sir. I know so much about the house. I could make myself useful."

"Ah, yes, I dare say. Well, I hope they'll appreciate the place and possess sensibility as well as millions."

"But, say!" said Van Elsen, coming to life. "Do you stop here all alone in this great place? At nights?"

She looked puzzled at his concern. "Why, of course, sir."

"With all these treasures? Priceless things. Good lord, it's like a gift to gangsters—to robbers and thieves."

She drew herself up quietly, and said with an exaggeration of her natural pride, "I have nothing to fear, sir. Nobody would think of it. You forget, you're in Scotland now."

Van Elsen nodded. "*Touché!* What a nation!"

Dacre had started the car by now, and Van Elsen hastened to join him. "Come on, Helen!"

"Thank you, Mrs. Memmary. I shan't forget."

"Thank *you*, madam," returned the old woman conventionally.

"What a character!" said Van Elsen as the car wound its way across the park. "She ought to be in a book."

"She was so good," said Helen, "and I'm sure she's very lonely and very poor. How much did you give her, Julian?"

"Ten shillings." He flushed. "Don't be indignant. I know we can't afford it, but I thought she earned it."

"I wish it had been a pound," said Helen.

"They call her Mrs. Memory," said Van Elsen with a laugh. "Good name, too. She must have been ' reminiscing ' for a full hour, Helen. What was it all about?"

"She was telling me about the family."

"The great days? I dare say they were great. But all that has gone; the world is moving towards universal democracy. I don't suppose Mrs. Memmary knows anything about politics."

"We didn't talk about politics," said Helen. "Just people."

"Look back," said Dacre, as the drive took a turn to enter the plantation. "There is your last glimpse of Keepsfield; magnificent residence to be let furnished."

"No, thank you," said Helen. "I don't like last glimpses of anything."

"Quite right," said Van Elsen. "It never pays to look back. If one believes in evolution, the Past has no contribution to make to the Future."

And so those three disappear into their own particular world, and it would seem as though the story is ended. If any reader feels that this is a fitting place to make an end he can conveniently do so. This is a warning. There is more to come, and you may not like it.

Will you risk the Truth, and read on? If you do you accept full responsibility. A story is not told unless it is told in its entirety; but that is no reason for forcing it whole upon a reader with a literary conscience. You may read no more; but if you must, well, then, you must.

1933

On a spring evening in 1933 a little elderly woman stepped off the Continental boat-train into Victoria Station,

London. She looked about her, confused, but there was dignity and not fluster in her bewilderment. A porter dashed up. "Luggage, lady? Taxi?"

"I only have this suitcase. Will you put it on a taxi, please; and tell the man to drive to some quiet, *good* hotel, but not—not expensive."

"She's a real lady," said the porter to his friend, waving away the taxi. "You can always tell 'em. 'Ear 'er voice, and look at 'er pretty little 'ands; and that soft, fussy black she wore, and them two white roses under 'er little chin. Poor, I expect, like all the real gentry. I know 'em. I was brought up in the country where there was lords and ladies."

Lady Rose was alone in London for the first time in fifty years. How different! How hard and bright and noisy, like Rome and Paris. She was glad she was not staying here, and that there was just time for a quiet dinner before the night train left for Scotland. Scotland! After fifty years. So long, long ago as a schoolgirl her heart had leapt and her eyes filled with tears as the train crossed the border, going home for the holidays. How would she feel now, an old woman of seventy-seven? Would the pounding of her heart not shatter her poor body, and the scalding tears blind those once bright young eyes?

She felt very tired after her long journey across Europe, but she could not—did not want to rest until she was in

Edinburgh again. The little hotel was in a side-street, a quiet haven where she could breathe in peace for two hours. She washed in the ladies' cloakroom, smoothed her soft, white hair, still curling, and sprinkled her hands with eau-de-Cologne, so divinely cheap in Paris. He soft, black clothes were made of cheap material, but she wore them daintily, and she had pinned two white lace gardenias at her throat with her last good brooch. Her little black hat was cheap, too, but it framed her face prettily, that face which still could smile with pink cheeks and pansy-blue eyes.

She had no desire for dinner, but she took some soup which was good, and a little fish and caramel pudding, and a cup of coffee. Then she left for her train in another taxi. This travelling was expensive, and she found she had not enough money for a sleeper on the Scottish express; but the porter was so kind, and found her a comfortable corner in a third-class carriage where she could doze through the long, dark hours.

Actually, she was sleeping at that great moment when the train reached Scottish soil. When she woke, bewildered for a moment, her heart leapt, and she almost cried out at the thrill. It was daylight, and she could see the gracious Lowland country and the Lammermuir Hills. Unchanged! Nature was the same; Scotland was the same in beauty.

Then the train was drawing into Waverley Station. Oh, was this Edinburgh? What a hustle; what a bustle! Not like London and Rome and Paris, she prayed; not Edinburgh, she couldn't bear it. Then her heart was gladdened by the sound of the soft, Lowland tongue.

The porter saw that she was old and alone, and a bonny little Scots lady. He directed her to a small, oldfashioned, family hotel in Princes Street; and there, fifteen minutes later, she was standing at her bedroom window saluting the past, the present, and the future. She had heard a bugle call from the Castle Rock. Years seemed to fall away from her as she stood erect; her eyes were shining, her heart was brave.

"Will ye take br-reakfast in yer r-room, madam?" asked the bright-cheeked maid.

"Oh, yes; please!" said Lady Rose, eagerly. Old Edinburgh below her window, so much changed and yet so dearly, so eternally the same. New, fascinating, glittering shops and electric trams and shining modern motor-cars; but the same Gardens where she had met her love, and the same brooding, magnificent, immovable Rock crowned with battlements against the limpid blue of heaven. Her eyes devoured Edinburgh; she breathed it, fed her spirit with it, and felt it tingle in her veins. It seemed only yesterday that a little girl in white had driven with Mamma in a carriage behind the Queen, while the guns boomed joyously from the Rock and Princes Street was gay with flags; only yesterday that an older girl in black had put her two hands into the hands of her golden lad and whispered, "I love you." And still the bugles sounded sweet and far, and the Castle sailed high in light, and the lilac mists curled round Arthur's Seat, and somewhere among those dim roofs lay Holyroodhouse sleeping her royal sleep.

"Oh, dear God!" whispered little, old Lady Rose.

It was easy to find her lawyer's offices for they were close at hand in George Street. The second Mr. Crawford, of Crawford, Crawford, and Nicholson, was as surprised as any family lawyer can be surprised. He was a young man of thirty when she went away; now he was eighty and one of the ancient monuments of Edinburgh. His father, who had known the Earl and the Countess, had been dead for twenty years. They faced each other, these two old, old people, across a musty, panelled room, with worn red leather chairs and a desk loaded with papers.

Word went round the offices. "Who do you think that is? It's the Countess of Lochlule; she who ran away fifty years ago with a clerk out of Hanover Street. Yes, yes, that's the one. She's Countess in her own right because her father, the old Earl, left no heir. Him? He's been dead for generations before ever she went away. Where's she been? Why, living in Italy with her husband, the ex-clerk. Where's he? How should I know! Oh, wait; he's dead! I remember now, died three months ago. Yes, she owns Keepsfield; magnificent old place, but it has been empty for years; it'll be a hoary ruin. And what a park! Miles of it. Talk about the good old feudal days; well, I'm no socialist, but really! Yes, Lady Rose Targenet she was. Quite a girl when she ran away, about twenty-nine, and now she's nearly eighty. But she's still pretty in an old-fashioned way. Poor old soul, she's not too well off. The estate has gone to rack and ruin, taxed out of existence. The park is rented in lots for pasture and pheasantries, but it doesn't bring in enough to keep the house in repair. She's got about four hundred a year. I know, because I used to send the quarterly cheques out to Italy. Do with the place? Oh, I suppose it'll be turned into a hotel or a girls' school if she can get anybody to buy it. She can't keep it herself, that's a sure thing. The old days? Oh, well! All the landed gentry were living in luxury then. I'll bet her father had fifty thousand a year, or more. Times change and things are more evened out in these days; not so much of the high and the lowly. We all get a chance."

Upstairs the old lawyer, still known in his native city as one of the shrewdest of his profession, was saying, " Won't you sit down—Lady Lochlule? We hardly expected to see you in Edinburgh again."

" What else could I do?" said Rose. " There was nothing left in Italy when he was gone. And call me Mrs. Montmary, please." She smiled. " One can't be a Countess on four hundred a year."

" Ah, you realize——" The lawyer coughed discreetly.
" You have been out of Britain so long. The old families
. . . the land taxes . . . heavy duties . . . after the war."

She smiled again faintly. " I understand. I heard of
English and Scottish friends; other families. It has all gone
down. Tell me about Keepsfield; is it the same?"

" We have done our best to keep it the same, Lady—
Mrs. Montmary. The house is in a good state of repair,
and a great deal of furniture remains, and all the entailed
property. Of course it would be impossible to reopen it.
I suggest you try and let it furnished for part, if not all, of
the year. There are rich Americans."

" I see. Is that what others in my position have done?"

He nodded. " The Mauchers have turned Shirlwell
Castle into an hotel. It is doing well. Melroch House is a
school; and Lord and Lady Culling at Bluish are taking
paying guests."

" I shouldn't like paying guests," said Lady Rose.
" First of all I want to see Keepsfield. I shall go down in
a few days, when I am rested. It was such a long, tiring
journey across Europe. And alone!"

" Ah, yes." The lawyer looked embarrassed. " I must
hasten to—er—condole with you in your sad loss."

She looked up with a bright, startled expression. " Oh,
no, no; please. I couldn't grieve. It had to be some day,
our parting, and I would so much rather be the one to be

left. He would have been lost without me. And what happiness I've had! All those years in heaven!"

Mr. Crawford felt more embarrassed still. He was not used to emotion and distrusted it; and as for old Countesses of nearly eighty who talked like romantic girls——

"You can perhaps give me some information," said Lady Rose, "about my relatives."

"I'm afraid," said the lawyer, "that they are nearly all dead."

"Ah, yes. I've lost touch in all these years, and " —she added—" they never forgave me!" She gripped the ebony handles of her black silk bag. "There were the children——"

"Yes, yes." Mr. Crawford coughed discreetly. "You knew that Mr. Alastair was killed in the war—with the Black Watch? He was thirty-nine. His name is on the Memorial up at the Castle."

"A friend told me of that," said Lady Rose. "My children never wrote to me. Their father's people brought them up to think so very hardly of me. Children are easily influenced, and they very quickly forget." She sighed. "Perhaps you can tell me about my daughter, Mary-Jean?"

The lawyer fidgeted. "She is in America, I suppose."

"Where?"

"No one knows, Lady—Mrs. Montmary. She was

divorced, and then married an American racing man. She hasn't been heard of for twenty years. Of course, she—er —isn't young now."

"No," said Rose, staring into space. "She's a middle-aged woman—poor Mary-Jean. And Archie, my heir?"

"Ah, yes—Sir Archibald. He seems to be in excellent health. Divides his time between Redlace and his London house. He has a shooting-box at Braemar, too. You know he's in business? He's a Director of Chetwode-Finchley, the armament manufacturers, doing *very* well. I've got a few of their shares myself."

"I should like to write to him."

"Of course. If you write to Redlace the letter will be forwarded. He's probably in London now."

Lady Rose was on her feet, one hand extended.

"Thank you, Mr. Crawford; thank you so very much for looking after everything so beautifully. You are kind!"

"Oh! Lady—Mrs. Montmary—I—er—really—no, indeed!" He fidgeted and shuffled, and felt an unexpected warmth at his heart. He had heard a lot about her, that she was charming as a girl. Well, there was something in it; she was charming yet, and pretty, too. A taking kind of woman, soft and natural and bright-eyed like a little bird. Nearly eighty? Absurd!

Lady Rose went back to her hotel, and sat down in her room with her window open to the spring airs of Princes

Street, to write to her son. Who can describe the hopes and fears, the remembrances that she sternly crushed lest they caused a tremor in the firm little hand that guided the pen in such beautiful, delicate characters across the page?

MURRAY'S HOTEL,
EDINBURGH

MY DEAR ARCHIE,

This letter breaks a silence of fifty years. It is from your mother. You were only nine when I went away. I wrote to you from Italy, but you were with your father's people and they preferred that I should not correspond with you. Now you are a man and will understand all the things which are past and done; that I didn't desert you in my heart, Archie—you and Alastair and Mary-Jean—but I couldn't take you with me to Italy, and it was right that you should be brought up in Scotland on your own estates that your father left you.

Your mother is in Edinburgh again, Archie, an old woman of nearly eighty. If you knew how I wanted to see you! Some day soon they will usher into my room a handsome middle-aged gentleman called Sir Archibald Galowrie of Redlace and I shall say, " He's my son! " and see a rosy, dark-eyed laddie of nine in a white sailor-suit leaning against my knee. Do you remember Queen Mary's chair, and how I read to you about little Tom the chimney sweep and the sea-birds at Allfowlsness?

I am going to Keepsfield in a few days, when I have rested and screwed up my courage to face the sight of what was once—and still is—so divinely dear. It is all mine and will one day be yours. There isn't any money, I'm afraid, but just the glory and beauty of our great house, now fallen on evil days. I have seen Mr. Crawford the lawyer to-day, and he was both kind and helpful, but no! This isn't a business letter, and all that can wait. Will you write to me at the above address, or care of Mr. Crawford's offices? Do you remember me, Archie? Would you know me? Of course not; but oh, how I hope there is a little of the old *Me* left. I loved being young, and I don't want to be old, particularly in Scotland where there is so much beauty still to enjoy.

The waiter here tells me that at night the Castle is flood-lighted and hangs in the black velvet dusk like a floating fairy palace, gleaming white and too lovely to be true. You can't think how eagerly I am looking forward to this bit of modern magic. There is something to be said for this clever but rather frightening age.

A little, little good-bye, Archie, until you come for me.

With love from your mother——

She hesitated for a moment, and then signed the letter with the name she had not used for years, the name the Queen had given her—" Rose Lochlule ".

She rang and gave the letter to the maid for the post, and at once a lovely calm seemed to steal over her. She felt strangely happy, light, and free. She lay down on her bed, and soon the pleasant noises of the street faded to a murmur. She slept until evening.

Four days went by and she was still in Edinburgh. She had been to the Castle, she had been to Holyroodhouse, and to the Gardens, where she first met Morie Montmary. She had thought it would be hard to do these things; and instead it had all been lovely. Before, she had lived in a world where these places were only memories; now she proved them real, and their reality linked joyful hands with her memories and she was lonely no more.

All very different, of course. There was a War Memorial at the Castle which awed her by its beauty. In it she read her own son's name. At Holyroodhouse there was no descending from a carriage, while powdered footmen opened the great doors to let the white-clad, smiling girls in; she paid her shilling and mounted the stairs slowly to Prince Charlie's banqueting hall, and there paid another sixpence to join the little party through the state apartments. This was the room! And there the Queen had sat—only now there were two thrones—and there she and Ann Dalrymple had pressed back, nervous and excited, against the panelled wall, and the chaperons had stood here, and the beautiful piper of Cameron of Lochiel.

". . . This, ladies and gentlemen, is the Throne Room where the presentations take place when their Majesties are in residence. Turn your attention to the portraits on the wall . . ."

The little old lady in black seemed to be neither looking nor listening, and two eager American college girls wondered what she had paid her money for.

Afterwards, in the soft spring dusk, she had walked through the Gardens. There were new seats now, freshly painted. She found herself whispering, "It was here!. . and here!. . He said . . . I said . . . Morie . . . Rose . . ." She saw a pair of lovers gazing up—as *they* had gazed—as one by one the little golden lights shone out above the night-softened Rock.

She went back to her hotel and asked, as she had asked in the morning, "Any letter for me—Mrs. Montmary?"

"No, madam."

There was a green baize letter-board with strappings of tape, and tucked into it a large, square letter. At that distance she could read the bold handwriting . . . "The Countess of Lochlule, Murray's Hotel, Edinburgh."

"Oh!" she cried, with a quick, hot flush, realizing what she had done in her hurry; and she seized the letter under the surprised eyes of the clerk and carried it to her room.

So this was Archie's handwriting! Bold and unfamiliar, but still Archie's. Oh, yes; it was Archie's, because it had the address of his London club printed in blue letters on the flap of the envelope.

Wait—she would take off her hat and sit down in the basket chair by the window and read in comfort. She would push the cushion, so, behind her back, and open the window a little wider, and listen for a minute to the clang of the town, and have one more glimpse of the lovely, white, flood-lighted Castle sailing above the clouds.

And now, Archie!

" Will you tell Mrs. Montmary I am here. Mr. Craw-ford, her lawyer."

" Mrs.—er—Mrs. Montmary has left the hotel, sir."

" Left the hotel! When? Where has she gone?"

" She left early this morning, sir. She didn't give any address; but if you are Mr. Crawford, she left this letter for you."

" Thank you."

The lawyer sat down under a palm in the hall and opened the envelope. Inside, folded in a sheet of the hotel notepaper, was a letter addressed to the Countess of Lochlule. Mr. Crawford took it that he was intended to read this letter, and promptly did so.

THE HUNTSMAN'S CLUB,
PICCADILLY,
W.1.

Sir Archibald Galowrie presents his compliments to the Countess of Lochlule and trusts that she is in good health and finds her property in satisfactory condition. Sir Archibald wishes further to inform Lady Lochlule that he is willing at any time to communicate with her on necessary matters appertaining to the estate, but otherwise desires that she will not further presume upon their relationship.

Mr. Crawford frowned and looked extremely puzzled. Why couldn't the Countess have told him herself that she had heard from her son? He regarded the single sheet of hotel notepaper which he still held in his left hand, and read the one line:

I have gone to Keepsfield.

" And without even giving me a chance to warn the gate-keeper!" said the lawyer impatiently. He thought of sending a wire, but refrained. What was there to say? The Countess would let him know if she needed him. What would she do at Keepsfield, anyway, an old woman like that? There wouldn't be a bed fit for her to sleep in. The fact was, she simply didn't realize the position; she couldn't imagine her old home empty of servants, empty of furniture, empty of warmth; a vacant, abandoned shell of a house, only kept standing by the money that came in from renting the park. Well, she would have to find out, and a bitter blow it would be to the poor soul. Everything gone! What a vanished glory! Poor Countess; poor Keepsfield; poor Scotland.

The Countess had arrived at the great gates by bus about noon. The bus, having set down a rather weary-looking old woman in black, went roaring on its way along the sea-road.

The Countess took one backward glance at the sparkling sea and the spring clouds blown above the Firth by a boisterous wind; then she turned to those high gates. She felt so small, and they were so firmly locked.

She was hailed by a tall fellow from the lodge, who indicated a small iron gate set in the railing.

" Was you wanting in, ma'am?"

She inclined her head. "You are the lodge-keeper? Kindly conduct me to the house. I am the Countess of Lochlule."

The man was dumbfounded.

" Ma'am! Ma leddy!"

He went into the lodge then and called his father, an ancient man of ninety, but hale and active.

" 'Tis the Countess, Father; 'tis her leddyship! Whit can we dae wi' her?"

The old man knew her; she knew him. He had worked on her estate. Old Highland eyes looked into Lowland blue, with the awful sadness and understanding of age with age.

" There's naething ready for your leddyship."

" That doesn't matter. I only want to go to the house. I want to go home."

" 'Tisna verra hame-like."

" It is home to me. And please to call me Mrs. Montmary."

" Mrs. Memmary?"

" If you choose to say it like that. It's a long way to walk to the house, isn't it? But perhaps if your son were to lend me his arm——"

So leaning on a strong Scottish arm, Lady Rose came home. As they emerged from the plantation into the park she covered her eyes for a moment with her hand; then slowly drew it away and looked upon her home, the white palace like a pearl against the green trees. At this distance you could not tell that many of the windows were shuttered and that all were blank, that plaster was peeling away and statues had lost their features, and that the whiteness was not so fresh as once it had been. Lady Rose looked in a puzzled way at the pheasant coops and the sheep in their fenced enclosures, where once had lain the open park.

At last they came to the great doors. The gate-keeper opened them with his key.

" The fountain doesn't play any more," said Lady Rose.

" No, m'leddy. 'Tis an awfu' costly toy, a fountain."

Rose stepped into the silent, marble hall; silent with the emptiness of years of closed doors and untrodden stairs.

" Oh! There is Archie's head. The alabaster head that Hector was so proud of. A sculptor did it, an R.A. He came from London. I forget his name. Oh, but it's dusty; it's soiled!"

" M'leddy, wull I be waitin' of ye, or wull I be comin' back in aboot an hoor?"

Lady Rose looked at him over her shoulder. She had taken out her handkerchief, and was trying to dust the carved features.

" Come back by all means; and will you bring some food, please, and anything else I may need for to-night?"

"But—but, dae ye tell me ye're stoppin'? For the nicht?"

"I'm stopping—always. I'm never going away any more. I've come home."

"But there's naething prepairrit—nae servants, nae rooms! We werena tell't——"

"I can do everything that is necessary," said Lady Rose quietly. "I'm very tired now and I want to rest. I know the rooms "—she smiled with a touch of weary humour— "and if you will bring along some simple food I shall be quite satisfied for to-night. I will see you and your father in the morning."

"Verra guid, m'leddy, gin ye say so."

"I do say so."

The man withdrew rather anxiously, closing the great hall door after him. Lady Rose stood alone in the vast silence. She took off her hat which was pressing her brow, and quietly went on dusting Archie's head with her handkerchief. Sometimes she paused to look about her, and when she did so a look of satisfaction deepened on her face. It was so beautifully quiet here, and she had a great deal to do; it was cool, too, and somehow she felt tired no longer. Perhaps now that she was back at Keepsfield she would never feel tired again.

————Oh, never a doubt but, somewhere, I shall wake,
And give what's left of love again, and make
New friends, now strangers . . .
                           But the best I've known
Stays here, and changes, breaks, grows old, is blown
About the winds of the world, and fades from brains
Of living men, and dies.
                      Nothing remains.
O dear my loves, . . .

RUPERT BROOKE
(From *The Great Lover*)

THE LAST CHAPTER

WHEN the Dacres' car had disappeared down the drive, old Mrs. Memmary turned back to the house. It was five o'clock, the afternoon heat was oppressive, and she felt weary and drained of strength. She did not remember when she had talked so much as she had done to Mrs. Dacre; and the revival of those old memories was having its reaction in a two-barbed pain that dragged at her heart and head. She closed and fastened the big hall doors, for no one else would be coming to-day, and crossed the hall to a side door which led to the servants' quarters. On the left was a small bed-sitting-room, once the butler's, which Mrs. Memmary had taken for her own. It was comfortably furnished, and a fire was laid in the grate in case of a sudden chilly evening. First she took down a biscuit-canister from the mantelshelf, and, lifting the lid, carefully placed within the ten-shilling note that Mr. Dacre had given her. There was a little other money there already.

Then she washed her hands, filled a kettle, and set it on

the gas-stove, and spread a white cloth over the table. She was thirsty and badly wanted her tea. She laid out her china, very pretty, old, white fluted china, with a wreath of gold rosebuds inside the rim of the cup, and a worn silver knife, fork, and spoon. Then she went to the cupboard and took out a brown egg, but after a moment's consideration put it back. She felt disinclined to eat, but while the kettle was boiling she toasted a very thin slice of bread.

Even that proved difficult to swallow, though the tea was life-giving. She drank the first cup greedily, the second with keen enjoyment, and poured a third to stand beside her for occasional sips. Then she lay down on a comfortable red sofa—the kind of cosy, old sofa that serves its day and generation, and then passes on to years of blessed appreciation in the servants' quarters—and took up a book which she had borrowed from the house library. It was George Eliot's *Romola*, but to-night she found it wearisome to read. She kept reading the same sentence over and over again, without even grasping the sense of it, and at the end of an hour she had not turned a page.

At last she became conscious that twilight was changing to dusk. It was time she made her last round to see that all was well in the house. She took a flash-lamp and went out into the passage, along and through the swing-door, into the marble hall. Her tiny circle of light picked out familiar objects: the alabaster head of Sir Archibald Galowrie as a boy, the scarlet robe on a high-hung picture, the flash of crystal from a great chandelier.

Slowly she began to climb the stairs to the Gallery above. It was lighter here because of the long windows at either end; the furniture, the parquet floor, the picture-frames all shone with a soft bloom like moonlight, and all their bright, clear hues were gone, leaving them the colour of the dusk. She sat down abruptly in the nearest chair, Queen Mary's chair. It was much too large for her. Her hands smoothed and explored the blue velvet cushion on either side of her spare body, and then found their way upwards to the wide arms of the chair, where they rested, from elbow to finger-tip. Her head slid back and found a comfortable place against the carved and padded back of the throne-like chair.

Her eyes turned to the west window. She could see the dark tops of the trees in the park stirring a little in their leafy summits to show that they lived; stirring against the paling sky, where the turquoise had been transmuted to gold and the gold to primrose, and where now in that tender sea floated a few tremulous stars. The day was over; another day falling untarnished and unmarked into complete forgetfulness. The air was full of soft whisperings.

"Just one more moment, children; it's getting too dark to read . . . Keep your feet still, Archie, my dear . . . one more story? Well, which shall it be? . . . The old keeper lived all alone upon the Ness, in a turf hut thatched with heather . . . But he never minded the birds nor hurt them; indeed he minded but two things in the whole world, his Bible and his grouse; for he was as good an old Scotsman as ever knit stockings on a winter's night . . . on a winter's night . . . Come closer, my darlings, and we'll say good night to the lovely world . . . Good night to Mamma and Papa; good night to the flowers and the sea, and the Realm of Scotland . . . good night to my pony . . . and Colinby . . . and Duncan of Kirkobothy . . . Who was he? Duncan? Kirkobothy? . . . so hard to remember! . . . Good night, Archie . . . All of you . . . *All of you! . . .*"

At nine o'clock next morning the old man from the lodge limped up to the great hall door with a covered basket of eggs, bread, and milk. He had made it his daily task to carry these light provisions to the caretaker. For once the doors were not open, and this was unusual; for at this time of the morning he was accustomed to find the old woman at work with her mops and polishing cloths.

He set down the basket, and with the slow, laborious movements of old age—he was past ninety—fumbled in his pockets for the duplicate key. He unlocked the door and went into the hall. It held the stillness of an unawakened morning.

"Hey! Mistress Memmary!"

He made his way, slow and shuffling, to the caretaker's room. She must have overslept herself. But she was not there, though all was neat and the bed made.

He shuffled back to the hall.

"Hey! Mistress Memmary!"

His high quavery voice echoed back to him as he hesitatingly mounted the marble stair. A burst of sunlight, escaping from the clouds, flooded the east window of the Gallery.

Why, she was sitting idle in the big, carved chair; a spare little figure in black, looking out to the west window, away from the sun!

"Och, Mistress Memmary! What for would you be frightin' me?"

His old knees trembled; he touched her hand, and put his fingers to her eyes which did not see. He shook his old head, and pleaded. "Mistress Memmary! Ma leddy! Leddy Rose!"

But Lady Rose had gone so far away that even her childhood's name could not call her back to earth again.

If you have enjoyed this Persephone book why not telephone or write to us for a free copy of the *Persephone Catalogue* and the current *Persephone Biannually*? All Persephone books ordered from us cost £12 or three for £30 plus £2 postage per book.

PERSEPHONE BOOKS LTD
59 Lamb's Conduit Street
London WC1N 3NB

Telephone: 020 7242 9292
sales@persephonebooks.co.uk
www.persephonebooks.co.uk